THE GUNSHARP

Tombstone—a town that drew killers and killing like dead men drew vultures. They were all there that year—Johnny Ringo, Doc Holliday, the Earps ... and Will Carney. Carney, the drifter that even the toughest gunfighters were too smart to tangle with. But the Eggerleys weren't very smart. They trained their sights on Will Carney, and Arizona's biggest blood bath began.

THE GUNSHARP

William R. Cox

First published in 1965 by Fawcett Gold Medal

This hardback edition 1996
by Chivers Press
by arrangement with
the Golden West Literary Agency

ISBN 0 7451 4678 3

British Library Cataloguing in Publication Data available

Printed and bound in Great Britain by
Redwood Books, Trowbridge, Wiltshire

Chapter One

IT WAS QUIET in the Oriental, a pall lay over Tombstone, men spoke in low tones, walked carefully along their accustomed ways, or sat with thoughts turned inward. Will Carney dealt the cards, sitting up straight, watchful, a sleepy-eyed young man, tall and calm at the poker table. Three of the players were only partially interested in the game. Carney had the most money before him.

Doc Holliday said, "Open for five dollars."

"Play," said Simwell.

It was all slow and casual, as though events of great portent lay in the moment approaching.

"Play," said Horton. He looked at Holliday. "Wyatt's talkin' with the colonel, ain't he?"

Hatfield dropped out, waiting for the answer, folding his cards nervously. Holliday took out a kerchief and mopped his moist lips, ignoring Horton.

"Raise," Carney said, putting twenty more dollars in the middle of the table.

Holliday leaned back in his chair. His eyes were peculiar, feverish yet without life, piercing but without light. "Carney, I don't know about you. All afternoon you been betting into me."

"What do you mean, you don't know? You pay to find out." Carney smiled without mirth, without meaning. "That's the name of the game."

"You teaching me the game?"

"Looks like it," Carney said. "You want to buy cards?"

Holliday flicked twenty dollars into the pot. "I want to look at one card."

7

"Maybe some of these other gents would like to see a card or two," Carney suggested.

"The hell with them," said Holliday. "It's you I'm after."

The others made hasty disclaimers, tossing in their cards. Carney regarded them one by one, shaking his head, then said, "All right, Doc. Here you are."

He peeled one off the top, moving so slowly that everyone could be sure. Then he laid two cards before his own stack of money, separated two from his hand, ground in the draw.

Holliday said, without looking at his hand, "I'll bet you a hundred."

"You had 'em going in," said Carney, sighing, dropping his heavy lids as he peeked one by one at the pasteboards in his grip. "You really did."

"Then fold," snapped Holliday. He was having one of his bad days, and everyone knew it.

Carney waited a long moment. Then he said, "Doc, you're the best poker player in the West. I wonder what you'd do if you had these tickets?"

"Make your play, damn you!"

The others moved uneasily, ready to get away from the table, ready for violence.

Carney said, "Okay, Doc . . . okay." He touched his money, looked out at Allen Street, returned to his cards. He said, "I raise you a hundred."

Holliday grunted. He held the five cards high, reading them for the first time, now that his bluff had not worked, now that he had been forced. After a few seconds he put them on the table, face down, and said, "You're too damned lucky, Carney. I didn't fill."

Carney put his own hand in with the discards, mixing it so that no one would ever know what he had held. Then he picked up the money and began placing it neatly before him. Turkey Creek Johnson came walking fast, nodded to the group, spoke to Holliday.

"Wyatt wants you at the hotel."

Doc nodded. "Yes." He stared at Carney. "I'd have gotten you."

"Some other time," Carney said.

8

"Maybe. Most likely not."

He looked around the Oriental, at the mahogany bar, the long mirrors, the paintings, the wheels—all expensive furnishings. "It was a nice stay in some ways. So long, gents."

Doc followed Johnson out into the chilly March weather. The other players waited until he was out of sight, then began to talk all at once, like kids let out of school.

Horton said, "The sonofabitch, he could've answered me."

Carney gathered the money, put it in an oilskin packet, stowed it away. He agreed with Holliday—it had been a nice stay in some ways. He had come to town broke and he was leaving with a stake. He got up and went outdoors.

Sheriff Johnny Behan was across the street. Neagle was with him. There would be men with rifles out of view, and some would show themselves, some of the cowboys, the braver ones. Earp and the others were in the Cosmopolitan Hotel with their lawyer, Colonel Herring. There would be Warren Earp and Texas Jack Vermillion and Sherman McMasters and, of course, Doc Holliday. They were all deputized. It seemed as though everybody in town was a law officer of some kind excepting Will Carney.

He was wearing a loose coat and striped pants and the gambler's string tie on a gray shirt. He hadn't worked cattle for months, but he felt well, he felt strong enough, he felt confident enough. Never oversure, he warned himself. That was the way to catch it and wind up on Boot Hill. Just certain enough.

Betsy Gaye came bustling, a carpetbag in her hand. She'd been staying at the Mancia's house, working for Nelly Cashman, working in the restaurant, finally working at the Oriental, but not with the girls from 6th. She was not one of them, he knew. Maybe someday she would be, maybe it would come to that, but for now she was young and energetic and she had all the nerve she needed.

She paused, brown-haired, hazel-eyed, full-bosomed,

9

narrow-waisted, long-legged, with odd, slanting brows, saying, "I'm heading for Sautelle—up north. Right now."

"You told me yesterday."

"It's going to be bad here with the Earps gone. Mr. Clum says so."

"You sure they're going?"

"I know it for a fact. They've got no real standing in town since Virgil got shot. Colonel Herring says so."

"They've got a few people to kill," Carney told her. "They got Stilwell, but there's some others they want."

"I don't care. Tombstone is no good anymore. I've got a job in Sautelle."

"You keep on telling me." He was a bit sullen. For a while there, he had thought she might ask him to go along—there had almost been something between them. After he had downed Bud Eggerly, that was, because, among other matters, Bud had tried to abuse her.

She said, "Well . . . Good-bye, Will."

"Good-bye, Betsy," he said.

She hesitated a moment. They had not, after all, done more than exchanged words and glances. She was afraid of gamblers, he was afraid of entanglements. The little roseate cloud evaporated. She went hurrying on toward whatever her destination, he stood on Allen Street at the corner of Fifth and watched her go.

The cowboys began to show then, up and down, self-consciously carrying long guns in the town, looking a good bit like fish out of water, Carney thought. Some of them were all right, most of them were not. Behan, the politician, was making brags that everyone knew he would not carry out. Carney walked across the street and went into the lobby of the Cosmopolitan Hotel.

He was just in time to see them come down the stairs, Wyatt and Herring in front, then Warren Earp, then Vermillion, McMasters, and Johnson. They looked as they always did, tough and ready. They were a hard bunch, and no one ever doubted it. Wyatt's moustache drooped. He was out of sorts. He saw Carney and paused, moving apart from the others for a moment.

"Good luck, Wyatt." They had never been close, but

10

Carney had always sided with the Earps and Clum against Behan and the Curly Bill crowd.

"Thanks, Carney. You sure you don't want to ride with us?"

"I'm sure."

The tall figure of the gambling lawman swayed away, wheeled back. "There's a hundred damn Eggerlys. Or their damn cousins. You're fast with that gun, but nobody is that fast."

"Bud came at me, you know that."

"Everybody knows it. Even Behan. But he's dead, an Eggerly is dead and buried. They're feudin' people. You can ride out with us, why don't you?"

Carney's eyes were on the level of Earp's. "I'm not one of yours, not all the way. Why should I bring the Eggerlys after you? Doc wouldn't like it, neither would some of the others. You got trouble, I got trouble. Let's leave it go at that."

Earp nodded. "Okay. Just wanted you to know—I remember you been straight with me. You need a friend, you holler."

"Same goes," said Carney. They shook hands very briefly, then Wyatt led the others out onto Allen Street.

There had been shootings galore, but there was none today, nor would there be, Carney believed. Behan made his play, all right, calling, "Wyatt, I want to see you."

But Earp answered, "You may see me sooner than you like, Johnny."

And then they rode out. It left the town empty in a peculiar way. Behan looked as though he had, for the moment, lost his reason for being. The cowboys didn't want to walk around with rifles, looking silly, so they got out of sight as soon as they could. Carney lounged back toward the Oriental. It occurred to him that Betsy Gaye may well have been right, that Tombstone was played out. He had a room over on Third and a good horse in a stall at the Okay Corral.

He lingered, however, his wallet fat, no destination in mind. He went into the saloon and ordered a drink. The poker players were still at the table, but he did not feel like playing, he did not have the gumption for it, nor

11

for Sixth Street, nor for anything particular. He had not been inordinately fond of the Earps and he had always felt uneasy with Holliday, but he recognized the end of an era, a time of his life.

It had never been any other way, he reflected, looking into his drink. He thought of his room, the bare walls, the hard bed, cold in the morning, sometimes ice on the surface of the water in the basin. Yet it was clean and for a while it had been his only home.

Home? He had never known a home. His first memory was in darkness, the acrid smell of smoke in his child's nose, then the hard hand of the Apache squaw knocking him away from the pot of dog stew. How he came among the tribe he never knew. He had been there, that was all, until Sergeant Willy Akron, the Army scout, had taken him away to the fort.

There he had grown into the ways of white people, with Army trimmings, and that had not been so bad, but the regiment was transferred to another post, and the sutler, a drunken fool named Jolsen, had agreed to take care of the child. When "Willy" was twelve, the Apaches wiped out the Jolsen family, and only his early training had allowed the boy to escape aboard a paint pony to the Carney ranch.

The Carneys were all right, small ranchers in the Valley in southeastern New Mexico. Tom Carney was a man whose hobby was guns and how to use them. He spent a lot of money on ammunition, which should have been used to improve his stock, but he was a jolly fellow who never fired a shot in anger until the night the Moser twins had called him in the local saloon.

That had been the end of Tom Carney. It had also been the end of the Mosers, because Willy, then aged sixteen, had come in with his foster father's Remington rifle and laid for them and wiped them out. Then he had to run and he went eastward to Fort Worth, where the herds were forming and needed hands. He worked as a drover, hard labor all the way up to Dodge, and there had been this young loudmouth with a reputation as a killer, and then Tom Carney's training had proved itself, and

12

Carney had shot down another, and now his reputation was made, a bad day for him.

He finished his drink and took one last look at the Oriental, which signified luxury of a sort, and then he walked out and went around the corner to his room. He got out his bedroll and his saddlebag and began to pack. His memory would not quit. His past continued to unroll inside him, a succession of pictures that he did not want to see again.

After Dodge his name began to grow. They looked askance at him. "We know you're all right, boy, but that hawleg of you'n is too quick. Better move on, sorry, we just don't want no trouble."

Then he got in with that woman in San Francisco and learned the ways of the towns and did not have to wear his gunbelt and he learned to deal, too, but he did not like being a dealer and took to poker. One-eye Carter taught him how to keep his hands loose and smooth with glycerine and how to detect cheats and to use them in retaliation if and when called for. Everyone called him "Carney" and walked widdershins around him, and he finally had to kill a tinhorn called Faro Jim and then he left the woman, who was not, after all, his alone, and rode out.

He was, he found, a man of the Southwest, of the desert and the mountains and the hot sun. He prospected some and learned the Arizona country, north and south, and the years drifted away. But in each year, somewhere, somehow, there had been a challenger, and it had been necessary to shoot.

He sat a moment on the edge of the bed in Tombstone, packed and ready to go, and looked at his hands. They were strong and quick, but the skin was soft from the daily application of the glycerine. He had not used them for hard labor in years. He looked like "Carney," all right, the quick gun, the killer. He looked like the man the Earps and Holliday did not choose to cross but rather hoped would join them. He looked like the dealer who had been in the Oriental with Bat Masterson and Luke Short and had seen Short kill Charlie Storms and had observed that Luke ought not to wear his gun in his pocket if he was going to begin gunfighting.

Luke had said, "Carney, I never killed a man before. Only Indians. Carney, I don't like it."

And he had replied, "Nobody likes it. It's a thing that gets done before you know it."

And then they had got drunk together, and soon afterward Masterson and Short, not liking the political setup or the war between Behan and their friend Wyatt Earp, had pulled stakes. Now it was time for Carney to go and do likewise, he knew. He picked up his gear and went down the stairs. There was no one to whom he might bid farewell, his rent was paid, he had no friend in the boarding house.

On Allen there was the usual boy eager to run errands, and Carney gave him the bedroll and saddlebag and sent him to the Okay Corral. He moved slowly, his hands swinging free, which was habit, and because he was what he was. It was seldom that he thought of this, and he did not like to believe it now. He was not an aggressive man, he never thought of himself as a gunfighter. He had no desire to engage in a duel with pistols, not then, not any time.

On the other hand, he knew that he was unlike other men in some ways. Life with the Apaches had blunted fear of death, had instilled a fatalism in him and perhaps removed any tendency toward guilt insofar as shooting a challenger was concerned. He had been forced to make his own decisions about right or wrong in a time when a man lived with a creed simple to follow. Give everyone an even break and never shoot anyone in the back.

There was a fallacy here somewhere, but Carney was not equipped by training or instinct to detect it. He only knew he was uncomfortable with his reputation and unable to shake loose from it. He walked eastward toward the stable, crossing at the intersection of Fourth. He saw Johnny Behan hustling toward him and waited, frowning a little, filled with a sudden premonition of trouble.

The little sheriff said, "Carney, just a minute."

"All the minutes you want," he replied. There were

14

people on the street, but they were going about their business, heads down, preoccupied. The sun was pale, and off to the north the Dragoon Mountains marched in the clear air.

"Glad to see you didn't ride out with Wyatt. Those bastards are going to get it before they make it out of Arizona, you can believe that."

"Maybe."

The sheriff said, "I can make you a deputy, if you'll come with us. We could use you."

Carney said, "Sorry, Johnny."

Behan stepped closer. "There's two of the Eggerlys in town."

"You sidin' the Eggerlys?"

Behan shook his head. There was no one within a hundred feet of them, but he lowered his voice. "They're bad people to go against. I liked the way you handled Bud, I'm tellin' you the truth. He was a no-good trouble-maker. All the Eggerlys are Kentucky backshooters. But there's a passel of 'em. They multiply. They're all over Arizona. If you was to take a badge from me, you'd have guns on your side."

"Like Indian Charlie?"

Behan looked reproachful. "Now, Carney you stayed out of it so far. Don't start hintin' at things you don't know for sure."

"I know that crowd murdered Morgan," Carney said. "I don't hold with bushwhacking. No offense, Johnny."

The politician's ease rested smoothly on the sheriff. "No offense taken, Carney. I had to try. Ringo likes you."

"I don't like Ringo."

"Sometimes I ain't crazy about him, neither." Behan sighed. "Sometimes I don't like a whole hell of a lot of things. Anyway, there's these two Eggerlys, leastways one's an Eggerly, the others a cousin, a Frazer. You deserve a fair deal." He hesitated, then said, "That gal, that Betsy, she's all right, too. Bud was pushin' when he messed with her."

"I'm leaving town," said Carney. "I don't want any trouble with anybody."

"You watch it," Behan insisted. He turned and

15

sauntered away, smiling at a businessman acquaintance who stopped to speak with him. Carney shrugged and continued on his way to the stable. There would be Eggerlys or their counterparts wherever he went, he thought. It wasn't a happy circumstance, but he had found no way to do anything to prevent it.

He had, it was true, not been one of Wyatt's men, nor had he been sympathetic to Behan and the "cowboys." Both, he believed, were out to feather their nests. Wyatt had an interest in the Oriental, and his authority had been only through his Federal connections plus Virgil's job as police chief. Virgil was shot down, crippled, but the Earps also had Clum and a vigilante committee of sorts on their side. Johnny was a politician who could get votes, and in the end it had to be the sheriff who won. But what did he win? Not much, thought Carney. There was going to be a change, and it would be Behan's turn to get out.

The Okay Corral was just ahead, and he remembered that fight and the furor it caused, the beginning, in fact, of the end for the winners. Nobody wins, ever, he repeated, it's just a merry-go-round and devil take the hindmost. He glanced up at Fly's photograph gallery, where Ike Clanton had fled, thus disproving the accusation that Wyatt and his crowd had meant to murder the old man, for they could have got him easily as he ran. It was all a big ado about very little.

He turned in the gate and then he saw them, the Eggerly man and the Frazer boy, ordinary men in Levis and dusty boots. One was on his left, the other on his right, and they were waiting for him. He saw the white, scared face of the kid to whom he had entrusted his gear and the stableman's flying bootheels as he ran for cover.

Then Eggerly called, "Carney!"

"That's me," he said. There was nothing to do but stand there and take it. He was careful to keep his right hand away from the gun butt. He knew too well how far away to keep it and how to use it when needed. They did not know this, of course, could not and probably would not have believed it did someone tell them.

16

The sun was high above, which gave him good perspective. They were just young fellows from the huge Eggerly ranch, cattle hands, with horny palms and thick muscles. They had never spent hours and days with old Tom Carney and his hobby. They had not been in shootout situations up and down the land. They did not have sense enough to fire upon him as he entered the gate.

"You kilt Bud Eggerly."

He did not reply. His instinct had taken over, and he was estimating which was the most dangerous. They had been too stupid to bring rifles, they were bound in the tradition of the six-gun. They wore their weapons low—too low, perhaps. They were crouching, facing him. It was possible they did not enjoy this, two men tackling one. There were more evil Eggerlys in Arizona than these two, thought Carney, even as he moved.

They had expected him to answer, they may have expected him to parley, to try for peace, even to beg. They were simple young men from the outlands. When he drew without making a gesture or saying a word, they both tried to get out their weapons at once, certain of their plan of trapping him in crossfire.

He shot the Eggerly in the middle, folding him like an old potato sack. He swung the gun barrel around, and the Frazer boy had cleared his Colt's. Carney took aim.

Then Frazer fired. There was not even a bit of wind from the bullet, so far apart from its target did it go. Carney held steady on the chest as Frazer triggered again. He pulled down, gently pressed, saw the dust rise from the boy's vest. He stood there, people coming from behind, voices calling, the stableman yelling for the sheriff. He reloaded the six-shooter and shoved it into his holster.

He uncovered his saddle, shook out the blanket, went to the stall where the horse called Star, a steady black with a white mark on his nose, was ready and waiting. He saddled up and found his gear and stowed it with plodding care. He found his rifle where he had left it after the last cleaning and placed it in a scabbard and attached it to the saddle. Then he led Star out into the sunlight.

17

Behan was waiting for him, a small, tentative smile on his bearded face, sweating a little. "Got to take you in, Carney. You know how it is."

"Maybe I don't want to go in," said Carney.

Behan said rapidly in a hoarse whisper, "You got to come in. It'll be all right. But you got to let me make the arrest."

"I don't got to do anything of the kind," Carney told him. "But I wouldn't want to get you in trouble with the Eggerlys."

He saw the boy peeking around the corner of the corral fence. He hesitated, hating to lead Star down the street, knowing the horse resented being led.

Behan said, "I'll take care of the horse. Trust me, it'll be all right, I tell you."

They walked through the gathering crowd. A rider spurred out in the direction of the Eggerly home ranch. Behan moved faster, taking two short steps to Carney's one long stride. They went into the office, and Behan scribbled on his calendar. People waited outside.

Carney said, "I plead self-defense."

"I'm puttin' it all down. Now, gimme your gun."

"Oh, no you don't," Carney said.

"There's people looking in. Put it on my desk."

Carney looked out the window and saw that Behan was right, people were watching. He slid out his gun and put it on Behan's cluttered desk top. Then he did not move beyond arm's length from its butt.

Behan said, "We'll go in back until they go away."

He turned so that his own holstered gun was easy to Carney's reach and walked toward the cells. Carney moved with him. Behan closed the door and leaned against it. He was breathing very hard, not a brave man but one who could keep his head in an emergency and thus save his hide.

"Now, listen, Carney. I'm going out and talk to those people. Your horse will be around back. I'm not tellin' you what to do, but I'm not going to lock this door. Just use your head, will you."

"I'll try."

"You've been decent around Tombstone," Behan

18

went on. "You did what you had to do. If you need a friend any time, call on me."

Carney said, "Thanks, Johnny," and watched the sheriff of Cochise County go through the door and out onto the street. After a moment, since Carney was now out of their view, the eyes vanished from the windows. He went into the office, picked up his six-shooter, put it in the holster, returned to the rear of the building, and cracked the back door, peeking out. There was no one but the scared boy and Star.

He gave the boy a round dollar and threw a leg over the black horse. He waited a moment, wary of ambush. Then he rode out and over to Fremont Street, which was deserted. He turned westward and heard a train whistle in the distance. Betsy Gaye would not have made that connection. She would be on the later train for Tucson.

He shook off thoughts of the girl. There would be a pursuit, and then there was Wyatt and his crowd and also Curly Bill Brocius and Johnny Ringo and that bunch. He would have to lie low and do some night riding if he did not want to be observed.

There was another alternative. South, across the border, there was a Mexican town called Mantocloz, just a little place in the sun. Nearby was a ranchero owned and operated by a man named Riley, long since a Mexican citizen. Once, in San Francisco, it had been possible to do a slight favor for Riley in the matter of a cheat at poker. There was always a place for Carney in Mantocloz.

It wasn't time, he knew. He had a destiny to follow, maybe to the end of a smoking gun in the hands of an Eggerly. He did not know why, did not question why. He only knew that he would ride northward.

He had not mentioned to Betsy Gaye that Cork Farber was in Sautelle, a hard man but a knowledgeable one, who had need always for a dealer or a rider—and often for a gun. Carney had never yet hired out as a gun, but he knew the necessity might come to hand, and if it did, he would be wise to be near ready employment.

He rode until he thought it time to make his cold camp. There was coffee and hardtack in his pack. The night turned cold, and the blanket felt good around his shoulders as he sat against a rock on the edge of the desert. This was the lonely hour.

Killing the two men in the fashion in which it had been accomplished did not harass him. Leaving Tombstone with the Eggerlys after him was just another piece of the life he had not chosen but which he pursued because there was no alternative. The girl, Betsy Gaye, did not bother him.

It was like a bad dream in which he was half awake. It was the counting: Whenever he had to shoot a man, he suffered from the same waking nightmare. It was the counting, he could not stop himself from counting, starting back with the Moser twins.

And he never could finish. Sleep or something inside him, or something half in the dream, half in his own mind, prevented him from ever completing the score.

He heard the sound of horses then. They were coming from the north, and he remembered that there was an Eggerly holding in that country. He threw the saddle on the black horse and waited a moment.

The sound increased, and he realized he was on the line with Tombstone and that they would be fanning out soon, since they could more or less correctly estimate his rate of travel. The news had traveled fast.

He mounted and rode toward Tucson. He could sell the horse and take the stage and follow his nose—and the girl—to Sautelle. All he needed was a little time, and Bob Paul, the sheriff of Pima, was a friend of Wyatt and knew Carney and all about the Eggerlys.

The counting in his mind ceased with action. He pulled up his coat collar and spurred the black horse.

Chapter Two

Betsy Gaye sat in a Mexican restaurant and ate frijoles with dainty fingers, smiling across at the ancient driver of the stage northward to Sautelle. It was very hot in Tucson for a March day, much warmer than yesterday in Tombstone. The sun was high and seemed to be getting ready for the coming springtime.

Abe Fuller was stout, short, clean-shaven, pink of skin, and white of mane. "You'll excuse an old man's talk. It ain't often I get a chance to sit with a young lady and wag my chin."

"Well, we both know Will Carney," she observed, wiping her hand on a checkered napkin.

"A man with no luck."

"I don't believe in luck. Bud Eggerly was looking for trouble. My father was shot for the same reason, he was a man went looking for it. I know about those things."

"And a shame it is, a young girl like you." He finished his frijole and stared at her. "The country's fillin' up. You should be settlin' in a home, not goin' for a job with the likes of Cork Farber."

"Carney is a decent man," she said, ignoring the advice, drinking a glass of red wine. "It's not right."

"Maybe so. It's not right they ain't got a replacement for my busted whiffletree in a town like Tucson, neither. But here we are, behind in the schedule, and who'll get the blame? Me. I know about luck."

"You knew Carney in Colorado?"

Fuller said, "In Denver. A wild town, don't go near it, no place for a decent girl. There was a man named Brown, a big galoot. He kept changin' the play on the

21

faro layout. Carney warned him. But they want to go up against a man like Carney. They get a couple of drinks, and it seems like a good idea. They want to take his reputation and carry it in their name."

"Carney killed him?"

"Shot him in the jaw. The man died. Gangrene, it was. Carney was long gone by then."

"But you said Brown started it."

"Man gets a name like Carney, people are either scared and stay away from him, or they go after him. Take the Eggerlys, now. They'll go after him. They'll get him, sooner or later, if he don't leave the country. But Carney won't leave."

"No. He won't run."

"He'll move around and duck a little and hide a little. Then he'll get cornered and kill someone, then away he goes. Not runnin', just movin' on. Would you believe I been on the frontier forty years, miss?"

"No," she lied. He looked seventy, he was probably fifty. His eyes were blue and watery, and his nose showed telltale veins.

"You got to remember, we don't have much law, even now. I mind when there wasn't any, nor towns, nor scarcely roads, 'ceptin' what we made ourselves or what the Spaniards had made before us. Carney, he come along a bit too late. They got the telegraph, they got railroads, they got all kinds of things. They'll move him into a blind alley someday and finish him." He paused and snickered, showing yellow, jagged teeth. "Kind of sweet on him, ain't you?"

"I wouldn't say that. He helped me, I'm interested in him." She was, she thought, telling the truth.

"He oughta head out of the country," Fuller said. "Not that I ain't got sympathy for him. I mind all the wild ones, and he ain't the worst."

"He's a gambler, not a thief. Doc Holliday can't beat him at poker. But he doesn't cheat."

"Whoa, now, don't mention Holliday to me. He is one of the bad ones. Miss, you shouldn't know all these things. It ain't right. Ladies should stay to home and mind the kids and all."

22

"When I have kids, I'll tend to them," she said. She smiled at him, though, for believing she was nice and for talking to her and listening to her. The waitress came, a dusky girl in a wide skirt of red and green and dirty white, and each paid for half the meal. Betsy's money was running low, and the delay wasn't helping. She followed Fuller onto the sunswept street, sniffing at the dry air of Tucson.

"Carney ought to go to old Mexico," Fuller was saying. "Or South America. Would you believe I been to South America, Brazil?"

"If you say so, I believe it." She shook her head. She was wearing a loose-fitting gray traveling dress and low-heeled light shoes to which she had changed that morning. She matched him step for step. "Maybe Carney thinks he has a right to be in this country."

"Right ain't might, no matter what the copybook says."

They walked slowly toward the stage station in the new part of the walled town among slower-moving, brown-faced Mexicans with white teeth and lazy smiles. There was a lot of adobe, and the ways were narrow, different from anything Betsy had ever seen.

She was disquieted, somehow. The sight of an Americano moving cautiously in shadows against a white wall did nothing to distract her thoughts from Carney. Yet she was not one to dwell upon the qualities, or lack of them, in a man of such slight acquaintance. She had been well raised until the death of her parents, she had been courted in the East Texas community since she was fifteen, according to the custom of the country.

She knew all the domestic tricks, she had tinkled on the harpsichord while strong young farmers sang, off-key, their affection for her. She could cook and bake and mend and iron and houseclean as well as any Dutch woman among those who had taught her.

She had been able to face the loss of her parents, her choleric father and tender mother, she had been strong enough to resist marriage when she had no desire for it, she had managed to exist this far, one way or another. No man had perturbed her as had Carney.

23

She knew gamblers. Her father had secretly lost the family money in the saloon where he had, finally, been killed. There was no time for preoccupation with one like Carney. She wished she could get him out of her mind altogether.

Or did she? It was best, she had found, to give honest answers to one's own questions. She looked again at the tall man who was entering a small cantina that bore a sign lettered only MURTINEZ.

Fuller stopped dead. "It's him. It's Carney."

"Yes, I thought so." She had not really recognized him, she knew.

"Why in tarnation did he come here?"

"The sheriff is his friend. Bob Paul."

"Bob's out of town. Sim Martin's the dep'ty. Sim's an Eggerly connection, a cousin once removed."

She took a step in the direction of the cantina. Fuller seized her by the elbow, pulling at her. "No, you don't. This is a time to git."

"No," she said. "No." She tried to break away.

It was too late. Men came stalking, their rifles ready. One had a star on his vest. He was fat and oily, and his lower lip was pendulous, and he was dangerous. There were six of them, covering the narrow street. A small dog ran among them, and Martin kicked him without rancor, his lip wet, his small eyes bright with searching.

Fuller said, "If he shoots it out, we'll be in trouble here."

But he was fascinated, as was Betsy Gaye, wondering if this was the ending, if here and now Carney would find no way to go. They lingered against the side of a cool adobe brick building. Betsy's hands pressed hard against the corrugated surface, her breath came quick in her throat. She felt nauseated.

Martin was close to the cantina of Murtinez. A waddling, beshawled young Mexican woman came lurching through the door. Flies buzzed and settled on Betsy's arm, the sour odor of wine and cooking struck at her. She wanted to cry out, to prevent what was going to

24

happen, but she could not. Fuller was cursing in a low monotone.

The woman passed close to Martin, put her shawl aside, and muttered something. The deputy raised his hand, and all the men converged, their nostrils dilated, their gun hammers ticking. The woman went on. A dark posseman with a shotgun took a position alongside the door of the cantina, crouching.

Martin suddenly yelled, "There's plenty of us out here, Carney. I got a warrant, all legal."

The silence that ensued was excruciating. Betsy lifted her hands to her face. Her knees trembled, her stomach turned over, her eyes burned with unshed tears.

Fuller was whispering, "Give up, dammit. Don't push them. They want you to try them. They want to tell it around that they killed Carney."

Betsy prayed. She remembered him in Tombstone, yanking Bud Eggerly away from her, slamming him out of the Oriental to the street, all bright with anger. She had lied to Fuller, he was more than a passing acquaintance, he was an image of what a man could be if he had the chance.

Martin said, "It's an arrest. Come out with your hands high. If you don't, may God have mercy on your soul, Carney."

Again the silence, then Carney stepped out of the cantina and into the sunlight, his heavy eyelids veiling all expression, hands raised. The shotgun men stepped around behind him. Now he was trapped, Betsy knew, and doomed, too. They took his gunbelt, and he seemed naked, vulnerable to the gaze of the posse and the people who now came scuttling, as though from burrows, giggling, talking, pointing.

Martin gestured, and Carney walked ahead of his captors. The possemen relaxed now, laughing among themselves, dawdling, only the shotgun man and Martin alert as the procession marched down the main street to the office of the sheriff.

Fuller growled. He said, "That's it for Carney. They won't take him to the reg'lar jail. Martin'll find a way to kill him."

25

"Yes," said Betsy. She walked, following the procession. She had to see where they put him, what they did to him.

Fuller, trotting beside her, protested. "It's no good. I got to tend to the stage."

"You're on his side. You know it."

"I ain't on nobody's side. I drive the stage. This here is plain foolishment."

Her mind whirled with plans for rescue, notions of legal defense, nothing coherent, nothing sensible, she realized. She said, "I've got to see."

"They'll put him under the sod," said Fuller. "It's no good, Miss, no good a-tall."

The sheriff's office was not too far away, and at the entrance the posse disbanded, heading for the nearest saloon to drink and brag. Betsy waited across the street while the deputies took Carney inside. She was acutely aware that every moment counted, that they might easily shoot him and explain that he was trying to escape.

"Now's the time," she said. "While they're relaxed and sure of everything. Now's the time."

"The time for tarnation what?"

"To turn him loose."

Fuller said, "Miss, you're plumb loco. De-mented."

"A horse. You'll have to find his horse and bring it around to the jail. You'd better ride him, then people won't pay any attention. You get it and bring it here, and I'll go inside only when I see you're coming close on the horse."

"You are talking like a loon."

"Maybe. I'm not sure. I won't let him die like this, murdered."

"They'll throw you in with him. You ever see one of these Arizona hoosegows? They got rats as big as cats."

She looked at him. "You're going to do it. Why stand there and argue?"

He knew she was right. Every instinct told him to run, to get to the stage, which was certainly ready by now and waiting for him. But he knew about women,

26

a lot more than people would suspect. His past had been studded with them, and he had great warmth and sympathy for them in this man's world of the West. He drew a deep breath and then spoke rapidly, as a different man, a younger man, decisive.

"Now, just a minute. You can't go bustin' in there and do him any good. We got to study on this a little."

"All right. But hurry." She was afraid that any moment they might hear the shot that would wipe out Carney and her own sharp, bright present as opposed to yesterday's uncertainty.

There was a wooden awning outside a small green store, and they stood among the peppers and tomatoes, watching the door of the office of the sheriff. The flies buzzed, two half-naked children chased the mongrel dog that had suffered Martin's toe in its ribs.

Fuller said, "That Murtinez. He must be a friend of Carney's, else why did he go in there?"

"You think he might know where Carney left his horse?"

"It's worth tryin'. I ain't much of a thief, always manage to get caught. Carney's black horse, now, that's another matter."

"Black with a mark on its forehead," she said. "A big horse, named Star."

"Horses don't know their names nohow," Fuller said. "I'll go and ask."

He sauntered to the cantina, eased through the door as though in search of a drink. Once involved, he was going to be good, she realized, he was an old-timer with vast experience. She waited breathless until he came out again.

He looked across at her, nodded, lifted one hand. Then he ducked into an alley alongside Murtinez' place. At the same time Martin came out onto the street and walked rapidly toward the saloon where his posse had gone for refreshment.

Betsy's mind ticked like a metronome. The dog came around again, the children in noisy pursuit. Mexicans strolled past her. She gave Fuller some time, knowing

27

that the black horse could not be far away. Then she could not bear waiting any longer.

She picked up her long skirt and walked through the white dust of the street. She went into the cool dimness of the office, leaving the door, by design, partially open behind her.

For a moment she could only see opposite her a thick, oaken portal studded with iron hinges, bolted with round, strong, thick tongues of the same metal. Then the deputy stepped from behind the street door, holstering a pistol, smiling, removing his sombrero, bowing. His hair was wavy and held in place with some kind of oil, his teeth flashed.

"Señorita. Pardon, please. It is that we have just capture' a dangerous creeminal. We must be ver' precise, you sabe, no?"

"Oh," she said, fluttering her eyelids, mincing, "I am sorry. I was confused, you see. I am a stranger here and somehow I am turned about. Around . . . I am lost."

"Ah, señorita, it is ver' easy to be lost in this, our old town, no? Where is it you wished to go to?"

She knew at once that despite his smiling courtesy he was dangerous. The greasy hair grew low, his eyes were wide apart, snapping black, filled with lively intelligence.

She made a weak gesture toward the door leading onto the street. "I forget which way I turned . . . and that little dog and the children, they run around so, it makes me dizzy, rather. I just want to get to the center of town."

He bowed again. "Deputy Sanchez at your service, señorita. If I may direct you?"

He went ahead, perforce, as she backed away to allow him to lead her out of the office. She could not seize a gun and put it on this man, she was well aware. She saw Carney's cartridge belt hanging on a wooden peg, but that was no good. She could not unbolt that great door. She would have to depend upon Fuller if anything was to be done. She was furious at herself, her eyes flashing around the room, seeking a way out. She saw a

28

half-opened drawer and caught the gleam of metal as her vision became clearer in the darkness.

Then there was a great hullabaloo in the street, and the dog was back, this time accompanied by a friend and pursued by a whole pack of shouting, tumbling children of both sexes and all sizes. She stepped quickly close to Sanchez and cried out in pretended fear.

"Oh, they frighten me, they do!"

Gallantly he strode toward them. She stayed close, managing, finally, to stumble against him, thrusting with her shoulder. One of the dogs yipped and ran between the deputy's legs. She screamed and stretched out her hands, so that again she pushed him.

He fell among them, yelling in Spanish. The confusion increased. She scurried back into the office, still protesting. She reached into the desk drawer and pulled out a .38 caliber short-barreled revolver. She made certain it was loaded. She thrust it into the wide sleeve of her gray dress and hugged herself, returning to the doorway, watching Sanchez dispatch the little mob with kicks and curses.

When he turned to her, she was all apologies. "I'm afraid of dogs, you see. When I was a little girl, one bit me, and I've been scared ever since."

He flashed his teeth at her, dusting his trousers, which were rather too tight. He said, "And now, señorita, the Americano town is yonder. Ver' close to the end of the street, which you will find there—on your right, no?"

"Oh, yes. Certainly. Now I see! It was the dog, I expect. Oh, thank you."

He retreated into the office, aware of his responsibility now, again bending at the waist. "Of a certainment, señorita. Adios!"

She walked to the corner. She saw Fuller then, on the black horse. She went close to him, as if inquiring further. She managed to extricate the gun and slip it to him as he leaned down to speak with her.

He said, "Murtinez had his horse, all right. But where in hell is his rifle? It's gone."

She said, "Maybe he lost it or something. Just get that gun to him. Can you do it?"

29

"There's a window," he said dubiously. "This is plumb crazy, y'know."

"Get him the gun, he's sure to know what to do. I'll see you at the stage," she said. She walked away, remembering not to look back. She passed the saloon where the posse was making loud noises of triumph, averting her face, ready to cry, not believing it would do any good, expecting a hue and cry when Sanchez discovered that the revolver was missing, wondering what would happen even if Carney did escape, if they would know that it was she who stole the gun.

She was not so brave now. She found the stage, the whiffletree replaced, the hostler growling that Fuller was probably drunk again, that the company would hear about this, that the world was a damn unfair place when a good man had to nurse horses and a bum like Fuller was a driver at twice the pay.

She crawled into the coach and sat in a corner. There was a drummer aboard, a sunken-cheeked young man with a bottle in his pocket. He drank from time to time, peering at her.

He said, "Name of Johnson. Cigars. Sell 'em. Glad to meet you."

"Don't be," she managed to tell him. "Just tend to your drinking."

"Stuck up, huh?" He sagged into the opposite corner, staring at nothing.

After what seemed hours, Fuller came to the door and looked in at her. He nodded, lifted one shoulder, then climbed up to the box and picked up the lines. The stage lurched, the horses settled into the traces, they rolled out of Tucson, northward toward Sautelle.

She would have wept had it not been for the presence of the cigar drummer.

Chapter Three

SITTING IN THE dimly lit room behind the office of the sheriff in Tucson with the .38 caliber revolver in the waistband beneath his coat, Carney thought back, his mind wandering a bit at times, wonderment in him. When he had heard the tinkle of the imperfect glass in the high window on the alleyway, he had thought it was his old compadre Murtinez risking his life in some mad scheme to turn him loose. When he had shoved over the bench, stood upon it, and recognized Fuller, he had been astonished.

"Shhh!" The stage driver had warned. "I'm a-settin' on your hoss, which Murtinez showed me where it was at. I'm puttin' it behind the cantina. Here's the only gun I could get holt of. The gal stole it, so look out when they come after you, they mighta missed it in the office. Where in hell's your rifle?"

"Lost it in a little ringadoo last night," said Carney. "What gal? How the hell did you get here?"

"Nemmine all that. Just take the gun and do what you can. I'm headin' out for Sautelle, and the gal's with me. I got to get scootin' before they see me in this here alley."

There really wasn't any more to be said. Fuller had put it all in a nutshell. Carney nursed the gun. There were five bullets in it. If they came shooting, he could die here and put an end to it. He had learned one thing very quickly—that he could not live in a prison cell. He did not quite know why he had surrendered, anyway. An hour or two had convinced him that a jail cell would kill him dead as a bullet and not so mercifully.

He had never before been incarcerated. The heavy

31

sound of the door closing behind him still rang in his ears. He had felt suffocated on that instant when freedom had been taken from him.

The strange flight and the brief fight on the desert had weakened his resolve, he supposed. It had been Curly Bill's bunch, he was sure of that. When Star had tired and he had holed up, he thought he recognized the man he managed to kill, Dan Hogan, one of the rustlers from down Contention way. There hadn't been much time. He had fallen over Hogan's leg, with bullets whistling about him, and thrown his rifle to keep from landing on his face. There had been no time to pick it up. This was a shattering experience for a rider, this was a tenderfoot stunt and it had contributed to his frame of mind, which was low when he sought Murtinez. He had slept only three hours, he needed a shave and a bath.

On the run, he thought, a man can't keep decent on the run. A pocketful of money means nothing when there's a posse with guns on your tail. Life means nothing. Maybe that's why he didn't put up a fight and draw Murtinez into it when they came at him. If he had thought further, he would have realized that Martin was an Eggerly man. Murtinez had told him Bob Paul was out of town, he knew what to expect when they took him in. They'd do it after dark, after they got some booze in them to nerve them up to murder, but they'd do it, and no mistake, because the Eggerlys were that way. They had land and power and they intended to make everybody knuckle under. They had to kill him because he had taken three of theirs.

He tried to understand why he had surrendered, knowing all this. He tried to figure out why he was now far from ready to give up.

Maybe it was because Fuller had appeared so unexpectedly, from nowhere, and riding the black horse, too. Always before when he had been on the run, every hand was against him. Now it seemed he had friends.

The girl, of course, Betsy Gaye, had been in on it. She must have been scared to pieces, stealing the gun. It was a tremendous thing for her to do. He had been right about her, she was someone special. When he got out of here—if he got out of here—he would ride after her and go to Farber in Sautelle and see what came of it. It was one thing to expect a lot, he decided, but another to hang around and let things happen if they're going to happen. It was different from planning, he told himself. A man like him couldn't plan. But he could let the cards run around and see where they fell.

He took the oilskin packet out of his boot, where he had put it upon riding into Tucson. He counted the money. There was over a thousand, it was enough. He replaced it, thinking that if he did die with his boots on, they would at least proclaim him a man of substance, might even get him a decent burial. The thought cheered him somehow.

Looking at it all from this point of view, he decided that life wasn't so awful, after all. Maybe that's all a man, even his kind of man, really needed, just someone on his side. You looked for help, you couldn't beg. If someone offered, then you could go on. It made a big difference. He had never looked at things like that before.

He heard them coming then. He had placed the heavy wooden bench, the only piece of furniture in the room, where it would angle off from the door when it opened. Now he moved it to the other side so that it would be behind their knees. He stood against the wall, taking out the revolver. He did not ordinarily trust nickel-plated, small-calibered revolvers, but this one felt like a cannon in his grasp.

Bolts shot back, there was a rumble of voices. Two or more of them, he knew. He wondered if shots would arouse the neighborhood and how Murtinez would act if they did and what chances he had of riding out. The door opened.

Martin entered first, a huge whale of a man. Sanchez was behind him. They had guns in their hands, ready to do the deed. The stench of whiskey was strong on them.

Carney said, "Whoa, now," and showed them the revolver.

Martin was so startled he dropped his gun to his side. Carney stepped past him and hit Sanchez alongside his slick-haired head before the younger man could shoot.

Sanchez fell inside the room, and Carney caught him with one hand and spun him into Martin. The two of them fell backward over the heavy bench.

Carney bent and picked up the Colt's that Sanchez had dropped. Martin lay like a beached whale, staring up at him.

"You . . . you goin' to kill us?"

"Not if you let go of that gun," said Carney. "It don't seem to be doing you any good, does it?"

Martin dropped the gun on the bench as though it were red-hot. Carney picked it up, stuck it in his belt. Sanchez moaned and stirred.

"Take his shirt off him," Carney said.

"His . . . his shirt?"

"Just rip it off, he won't mind."

The fat deputy made several attempts. He finally succeeded in getting strips of cloth from Sanchez' back.

"Gag him," Carney said.

Martin folded a portion of the shirt and thrust it in the mouth of his assistant. Carney made sure of the knot, put together the rest of it, tied Sanchez hand and foot.

"That's just for starters," he said cheerfully. He felt very good. It was fine to have that door open. He motioned Martin to his feet.

"We'll go find handcuffs and things," he said. "You ought to know where they are."

Martin waddled into the office. It was growing dark outdoors. Carney went to the desk, found what he needed. Upon inspiration he surreptitiously returned the nickel-plated weapon to a drawer, the right-hand drawer at a guess, knowing that Martin wasn't left-handed by the way he wore his holster. Now they might not trace it back to the girl, he thought.

In the detention room he manacled both men. Then he removed enough shirting from Sanchez to gag Martin. He surveyed his handiwork and found it good enough for the present. It would be some time before anyone came to check. Martin would not have advertised in advance the deed he had planned in that room.

He barred the door, wondering if they felt as he had when it clanged upon his back. He hoped so. He hoped they would have a bad time of it. He rather hoped he would see them again someday under better circumstances, two men who had planned to shoot him in cold blood.

He took his belt down from the wooden peg and felt fully dressed when he had strapped it on. He selected a rifle from the rack against the wall, identical to the one he had lost the previous night. He helped himself to some ammunition. Then he sat down at the desk, stuck forty dollars in an envelope, and wrote a short note to Bob Paul: *Sorry about all this but you ought to take care of what kind of deputies you hire. This'll pay for damages. Hasta luego. Carney.*

He put this note in the left-hand drawer and hoped Sheriff Paul would find it before the others did. He went to the door and looked out on the street. Guitar music tinkled in the distance, a Mexicano song which they seemed to sing over and over all the time—"La Paloma." There was no one in sight, only a mongrel dog sleeping in the doorway of the greens store.

He stepped out and walked slowly toward the cantina, trailing the rifle, whistling in tune to the guitar strains. When he stepped inside the saloon of Murtinez, he was sure he was unobserved. He felt light-headed and gay.

The proprietor was behind the bar, dozing. There were no customers in the place. Murtinez was a tall, oaken-faced man, a former bandido come to retirement in this quiet backwash. They had known each other along the border in Texas some years back. He had deep-set brown eyes and a wide mouth. He showed no surprise at Carney's sudden appearance.

"Amigo, it is good. I had thought of various plans, none of which would advance us," he said in Spanish.

Carney reached for the whiskey bottle. "The gal and Fuller did good enough."

"Your horse, he is out in the back. I would suggest you take the road south. Remember Mantocloz?"

35

Carney shook his head. "Not yet. Someday, maybe, but I'm not ready."

Murtinez drank from a wine glass. "The day will come. You are destined to run and run until you come to Mantocloz. It is a matter on which you should ponder, amigo."

"I've thought on it." He swallowed the whiskey. "Could I have some grub? It'll be a long ride."

"It is waiting for you," said Murtinez, showing many white teeth. He produced a hefty packet. "Go with God."

Carney put a bill on the bar. "And you, my good friend."

"You must not pay!" He thrust a gnarled brown hand at the bill.

"I have plenty. It is a time to pay." Carney waved his free hand and went out the back way and found Star tethered to a stake in a grassy patio. He tightened the cinch, stowed his food, put the rifle in the scabbard. There were stars in the sky now. It was quite dark. He mounted the horse and turned north over back streets he knew from previous visits.

They would be coming after him, perhaps. On the other hand, Sheriff Bob Paul would have something to say about that. The worst part, the inescapable threat, came not from Martin or Sanchez. It lay in the laps of the Eggerlys, that vast clan that overran this part of Arizona and New Mexico. The Eggerlys would always pursue him.

He was almost to open country when he heard the sound of many horses. He pulled over, dismounting, taking his rifle from its boot, standing beneath a pepper tree in the dark. They came into full hearing, a shadowy group, twenty or thirty of them. In the van rode two men of exceptional height. They were walking their horses, as though they had come a long way. As he watched, the leaders put up their hands, and the caravan stopped. Horses snuffled at their bits, pawed the ground, anxious to get to feeding. Gear squeaked, leather on metal.

Carney shifted his position, lining up the two tall men against the starlight. He recognized them then. He gripped the rifle tight, holding Star by the nostrils.

36

The old man was Simon Eggerly, chieftan of the clan. No one could mistake that prow of a nose, the angular jaw, the thick neck. With him was his son Paul, a brother to the late Bud Eggerly, another thick-shouldered giant.

Simon was saying, "We don't know whether Carney came this way or not. We don't know nothin' a-tall, come right down to it. Just talk."

Paul Eggerly said, "I got it from that Indian. He said Carney fought it out with Curly Bill last night on the desert. Them Indians know."

"They lie, too." The old man brooded, sagging a moment in the saddle. "You believe anything, Paul. Too bad it had to be Bud that got it."

"Now, Paw, that ain't a nice thing to say, is it?"

"Bud had more brains than any of you."

"Bud drank more whiskey and fooled with more gals, too," Paul said, half afraid, half defiant. "Bud got his death pawin' a gal in Tombstone, you know that's the truth of it."

Simon swung a long arm. His hand cracked against the face of his son like a whiplash. The horses wheeled in a circle. The men sitting their horses did not move or speak as Paul fought to keep from being unseated.

Simon Eggerly roared, "Bud was a he-man. He could drink and he could handle women. I want y'all to hear this: Carney killed Bud and Carney's got to be killed. I don't care where he goes—in this country, in Mexico, in Canada, down to South America. Long's I'm alive, there'll be Eggerly people after him. Now don't nobody never put down Bud to me again. We're goin' in and check with Cousin Martin and then we're spreadin' out and we're goin' to find Carney and we're goin' to bury him."

He rode into town, and the company followed him. The son called Paul brought up in the rear now. His head was sunk in his bull neck as he rode alone.

Carney marked him well. There might come a time when he would need to know all about Paul, who had sense enough to realize his brother Bud had been a town bum and a cruel womanizer.

37

One thing was certain—there would come a time when the Eggerlys would be there, and he would have to face them. He knew now, as he had sensed before, that Sautelle was no refuge.

Cork Farber might provide a stopgap, a place and a time to think things out. The girl might have another answer. It was a question of time and circumstance, he thought.

He mounted as the last sound of the horsemen was gone southward. He was going to ask a lot of his black horse this night. He was not going to get any sleep until the sun was well up. He was putting as many miles as possible between himself and the Eggerly people.

Chapter Four

CORK FARBER stood on a hill outside the town of Sautelle and talked with his friend and partner, Dr. Robert Reynolds. "It's raw and new, but it'll make a place to live in."

Reynolds said, "It's nice that you can visualize it."

There was one street, cut straight down the slope, running from the road that led from the ore deposits to the valley, thence upward again to the lowering mountains beyond and toward New Mexico. It was lined with raw, unpainted buildings, false-fronted and ill-made. To the south lay some fallow ground, tilled and dotted with cabins, where hard-handed farmers labored and raised more children than crops.

Over and beyond the farms was grazing land. Two large outfits shared the acreage, the *Flying M* and the *Ace-Deuce,* owned by Old Man Sharpe and Kit Christopher. Both were prospering.

The mines were properties of the New York Company and employed immigrant help who spoke little English but spent their money in any language. These were

customers for Cork Farber, proprietor of the biggest—
and only—saloon and gambling establishment in Sautelle.

He said, "The mines will pay off for twenty years.
By that time the farms will be producing, and we'll
have a railway spur, and the cattle business will boom.
I can wait, so long as the living is good."

"You have vision, true," murmured Reynolds. "I
wonder if you have the patience?"

"I can learn." He was a blond young man with slop-
ing shoulders and a narrow waist. He wore town clothing,
well-fitted, which he had tailor-made in Denver. His hat
was curly-brimmed, a pearl gray. He never allowed the
set of his garments to be spoiled by a gunbelt, choosing
instead to carry a sawed-off .38 in a specially designed
shoulder holster.

Doc Reynolds was, at thirty-six, ten years older. His
visage was saturnine, his skin colorless, immune to the
rays of the sun. He was a native of New York. He
customarily dressed in black, which accentuated his pal-
lor. His nose was long and sharp and slightly veined.
His chin receded into his white stock, his brow was high
and prominent.

He said, "Yes, you have learned a little but not
enough. You should be married, my friend."

Cork Farber flushed. "Sometimes you go too far,
Doc. There are matters best left alone."

"You're too rough on women," his friend told him
without heat. "It'll be your downfall if you don't mend
your ways."

"That's all over," Farber protested. "I don't want
to talk about it."

"Not that I care. People talk, you know. A saloonkeeper is a big man only so long as he obeys the natural
laws. Even then he is suspect."

"When the time comes to stop keeping a saloon,
I'll be in another line." Farber's eyes were bright. "Whatever is right for me, I'll be in it."

Reynolds nodded. "You have learned. In time the
bankers and lawyers and shopkeepers will rule the towns.
Bars and gambling are for the frontier. In a few years

they will be outlawed. Keep your head, listen to good advice, and you'll survive."

"Listen to your advice," said Farber. "That's all right. You've been right all along. We haven't done bad for a couple of easterners."

"Easterners? What else? Where did everyone come from? Certainly not here. There were only Indians here until easterners stole their land and ran them out."

Farber said, "The hell with the Indians. Should we go in for the morning's morning?"

"I thought you'd never suggest it," said the doctor. "So much philosophy at such an hour depresses me."

They walked down the hill to Sautelle. Each wore low-heeled boots, their gait not quite western despite their years on the frontier. They had come out together in '75 after dire experiences in New York City. They had met in the Tombs, as a matter of fact. Farber had been caught stealing, Reynolds purveying opium on a large scale. The latter had seen possibilities in the young lad and had bought him out through connections with the Tweed Ring then in power.

The medical man had not been wrong about his protégé. Farber had eagerly sought knowledge, had proven courageous and loyal. Reynolds had substituted alcohol for his favorite dream through smoke and managed to practice medicine up and down the new land, which so sorely needed men of his profession. They were a team, they worked together, first in New Orleans. It was there Farber acquired some polish and it was there he learned from the river gamblers how to deal from a cold deck. It was also in New Orleans that the first woman trouble occurred, which had precipitated the departure of the two New Yorkers.

Texas was crude and rough, but it provided new experiences and a place to learn the simple, basic rules of the frontier. Doc Reynolds always cautioned his young friend not to break these laws, in fact to proclaim loud support of them whatever the circumstances. Still, in El Paso Cork Farber had run afoul of a Mexican girl who tried to kill him with a poniard in a public place, and it was time to move on again.

40

They went to Fort Worth and thence to Dodge City, where they had stayed for a couple of years, laying low in that wild and boisterous town, carefully noting the ways of the men with the reputations. It was from Luke Short that Cork got the name of the Denver tailor who made his clothing. It was from Dandy Dave Cullen that he caught onto the shoulder draw with the .38 revolver. It was from Wyatt Earp that he learned restraint in public.

They moved again, always looking for a place in which to settle and grow with the development of the community. This was the idea of Doc Reynolds, who could see ahead to the taming of the frontier and who desired a place of security in which to retire to ease and comfort. In time Cork Farber learned the meaning of such a goal and concurred with its pursuit.

Sautelle had sprung up with the discovery of silver and some gold in the mountains of northern Arizona. It was not a big strike, it would never provide another Comstock Lode boom, but it was steady, and the New York people who put up the money, absentee owners, were satisfied that it had a future. The farms had already been there, the cattlemen came when Dodge played out to settle their herds on good grass in clement weather without the danger of Texas tick or hoof-and-mouth disease. The two adventurers had been on the ground early.

Now they could walk down Main Street and receive the polite, if not warm, greetings of the citizens who had come later to begin their commerce. There was D. Brand of the small bank, Ed Leeds of the General Store, Reverend Peterson, all the representatives of the law and order to come. All were solid citizens—and each had his own small idiosyncracy, some peccadillo from his past better concealed. Reynolds and Farber had been careful to discover these past indiscretions and to allow the individuals to be aware of their knowledge.

They came to the largest building on the street, the Cowboy Saloon, Cork Farber, Prop. The only law in Sautelle sat on the long, covered verandah in a rocking chair.

41

He rose to greet them, Marshal Dan Shriver, stout, pink-faced, squint-eyed, affable.

"Cork, Doc, howdy today?"

The three went inside the saloon, as was their daily custom at this time, before noon. It was a big room, with a piano at the rear on a small platform, a faro layout, two deal tables, and a table for monte. The bar was long and well polished by Chico the Mexican, a scar-faced, burly man with an olive skin and a thick mustache, who silently placed a bottle and three clean glasses at the far end of the dark mahogany, facing the door. There were doors leading off to other rooms and stairs going up to quarters above, where both Farber and Reynolds had apartments. They had built the place well, with an eye to the future. Sautelle would have to grow up around its saloon.

Farber passed the whiskey to the marshal, who filled his glass, then Doc's. Then he passed it to Farber, who poured a small drink and slid the bottle down to a spot at Doc's elbow. This was all part of ritual.

"Real nice day, gents," said Shriver. His voice had the tang of Alabama plus Texas. "Spring come early this year, I'd say."

" 'Buttercups and daisies, oh, the pretty flowers; coming 'ere the springtime, to tell of sunny hours,' " quoted Reynolds softly in a falsetto singsong.

The marshal grinned. "You're a somethin', Doc. You surely do grind me down."

Farber said, "Any news?"

Shriver drank, poured, sipped. He blew out his pursy lips. "Well, now, you might say so."

"Telegraph been busy?"

"You might say that, too. Busy as a bumblebee."

Reynolds and Farber exchanged glances. The marshal was the town gossip. He kept up a voluminous exchange of telegrams, at the city's expense, with every town west of the Rockies. He was coy as a kitten when he got hold of something juicy or something valuable to the three of them, and they were willing to indulge him.

Reynolds asked, "Anything about the mines?"

"Nope." Shriver giggled.

"Anything about the price of cattle going up?"

"Nope."

"Then, who cares?"

Shriver said, "Plenty out of Tucson. Tombstone, too."

"Did Wyatt kill another Clanton? Good job, if so."

Shriver blurted, "They done killed Curly Bill, that's who. And Injun Charlie and some say Johnny Ringo in the bargain. And they're headin' into Colorado. Johnny Behan's got warrants for 'em all. That's the end of the Earps in Arizona. I got it for sure."

Reynolds said, "They didn't take Tombstone, you see, Cork? They didn't last. They took some of the cream, but they lost the political battle."

"I was wrong," Farber acknowledged. "I thought they'd make it down there."

"Johnny Behan has his faults, but he keeps his finger on the pulse of the voters. It's a lesson to us all."

"Amen," said Shriver. "Uh—got another message. From Simon."

"Ah," said Reynolds. "Cousin-in-law Simon, eh?"

"He made it," Shriver said defensively. "He made it bigger'n anybody."

"Not up here. Not yet," Farber told him. "We don't need the Eggerlys up here."

"I know you don't need 'em. On th' other hand, could be they'd be a help when you did need 'em."

"Could be," said Reynolds. "Someday. Perhaps."

"There's half a dozen of us in this county now. You know that. We been here a long while, us Eggerlys."

"You mean 'those Eggerlys,' don't you, Marshal?" Farber swirled the small amount of whiskey in his glass. "It's your wife's family, isn't it? You're one of us, aren't you?"

There was a small pause while Shriver drank, poured again, drank again. Reynolds hummed a small tune. He had a light, surprisingly tuneful voice.

The marshal said, "Simon sent a message to look out for a killer. Fella shot down Bud Eggerly and some others. A real bad one. Simon's sendin' telegrams all over the country about this fella."

"That is Simon's habit. He doesn't believe in leaving

43

an enemy unharmed," said Reynolds. "Wasn't that last man you shot one of Simon's?"

"He was a thief and a killer."

"And you shot him on sight."

"With a rifle. From ambush," added Farber.

Shriver said, "I had a poster on him. He was plumb dangerous to Sautelle and everyone in it."

"Oh, well, that makes it different," said Reynolds with heavy irony. "No use to arrest and try a man like that."

"Certainly not," said the marshal. "I get me this Carney in my sights . . ." He broke off, sensing disfavor.

"Carney? Did you say Carney? Will Carney?"

Farber laughed. "If Carney comes to town, you'd better get him in the back. From a long ways off."

"We know him," said Doc. "At least we knew him. In Denver." He looked at Farber, nodding. "If he's on the run from Eggerly, he might head this way, at that."

"Colorado wouldn't be healthy for him."

"Nor for anyone who tries to stop him on his way."

Shriver said, "Now, hold on a minute. Are you tryin' to tell me this murderer is a friend of yourn?"

"Friend? Well, I don't know. What do you say, Doc?"

"Not a close, intimate friend."

"Then, he better not come to Sautelle," proclaimed Shriver. "Cousin Simon was right definite about him. Carney's number is up."

They ignored him, talking over his head as though he had suddenly vanished. "Do you imagine he's looking for a job, Doc?"

"If that gang is after him, he'll need what aid he can get."

"He's the quickest man I've ever seen."

"Probably the swiftest hands in the country."

"It would help the town to have him on the job."

Shriver wailed, "Now, wait a minute, here. What in tarnation you all sayin'?"

"He'd make a fine marshal."

"Honest, too. Remember how honest he is?" Farber asked.

Doc said, "How could I ever forget?"

Shriver begged, "Now, men, I wasn't aimin' to go against you all. I'm a Sautelle man, first of all. Cousin Simon, he runs things down South. What right's he got interferin' up here in our country and makin' trouble for me?"

They favored him with their regard. He squirmed inside his clothing, a sweating fat man wearing a star and a revolver that ill became him.

Doc said, "There's half a dozen of you, as you say. We wouldn't want Carney rubbed out, even by accident."

"No," agreed Farber. "And if we put a star on him, your people would think twice about bushwhacking him."

"Ain't nobody goin' to harm a hair of the head of any friend of yourn," said Shriver. "Nobody in this country'd dare do such a thing."

"In other words, you like your job," Doc said.

"Of course I like my job. I ain't altogether no fool, you know."

Farber smiled. "You'll have to prove that, Dan."

"I'll prove it. Any way you say. Just try me."

"You might try turning around and saying hello to Will Carney," suggested Reynolds. "He just tied up at the racks."

Shriver spun around, jowls quivering. He rubbed a sleeve across his mouth, his small eyes squinting. Will Carney pushed through the swinging doors and paused against the change of light.

Shriver squealed, "Mr. Carney, welcome to Sautelle. Come here and say howdy to a pair of your good podners. We're all plain glad to see you."

Chapter Five

THE BOTTLE WAS down another few inches. Carney felt empty, since he had not eaten that day, yet he was

45

also exhilarated by the friendliness of his welcome to Sautelle.

Farber said to Marshal Shriver, "Hadn't you better check on the telegraph company again? Wouldn't want you to miss anything coming over the wire."

Shriver wiped his brow with his fingers. "Reckon you're right, Cork. Yeah, I better go over there." He grinned weakly at Carney. "We keep up on things hereabouts. Hope you have a nice trip, the weather's fine for it all right."

They watched him leave. Doc Reynolds laughed softly on a minor note, pouring another large drink into his shot glass.

Farber lifted one shoulder, sighed. "He's useful. The farmers like him. The miners tolerate him. We only have trouble with the cattle people on a Saturday night. It's a pretty quiet town."

"He seems like an easygoin' galoot," Carney said. He wasn't thinking about the marshal, he was hungry. "Only I'm not thinking about moving on just yet."

"Good! Shall we sit down?"

They took a fresh bottle to the table. Farber was partaking of little, Doc was using a lot of it, Carney noted, struggling to keep his own head clear. They sat down, and he was aware of soreness from his long, swift ride through the country.

He said, "You might get yourself some trouble in the outlying districts, at that. You heard about Nok-e-da-klinne?"

"Nocky-who?"

"He's an Apache medicine man."

"There's no Indian trouble. They're quiet on the reservations, they're afraid General Crook will come back and haunt them."

Carney shook his head. "Not this bunch. Nok-e-da-klinne has got 'em believing in ghosts. They call him 'Fire King.' "

Doc said, "At Fort Apache they call him 'Fireboy.' He's a faker."

"The Apaches don't think he's a faker," said Carney. "I came across him last night. They were dancin'

46

up a storm. Apaches don't dance very much. When they do, look out."

"General Carr at Fort Apache will take care of him," said Farber. "Tell me, Carney, have you any plans?"

He shifted a bit in his chair, pushed the whiskey away. He said with diffidence, "Thought I might get a job hereabouts."

"Have you got trouble?" Farber asked.

"I've always got trouble, you know that."

"Anything you want to tell us?"

Carney said, "You'd hear it sooner or later. I got Eggerly trouble."

Doc said in his whiskey voice, " 'Tiger, Tiger, burning bright, in the forest of the night, what immortal hand or eye could frame thy fearful symmetry?' "

Carney was nonplussed, but Farber only smiled and reassured him. "Doc gets that way sometimes. He's full of poetry, Doc is."

"I see." Carney frowned. "I wouldn't want you to get mixed up with my troubles. I've got some money. It's just that I hate to run any more. Down South, there, the Eggerlys have got a lot of law."

Doc snickered, but Farber kicked him under the table and said, "I know what you mean. Well, we've got things going good up here. The town's not incorporated. There's a citizen's committee and there's Shriver—and there's us. We do all right."

"I expect you do your own dealing."

"I could use a man," said Farber. "I don't have a relief man. And, then, the cowboys. I could use a gun."

Carney shook his head. "I don't hire out my gun."

"I know that. But you do wear it," Farber said. "You can't take it off."

"I don't intend to."

"Then—you've got a job," said Farber. "A hundred per month okay?"

"Just fine," said Carney. He felt a great relief, and his hunger increased. He stood up as both men smiled at him. "Thanks. I'd better go and eat."

Farber leaped to his feet. "Why, sure. I'll bet you

are hungry. I'll go along—it's about time for the stage."

Doc Reynolds sat without stirring. He was evidently one of those drunks who retain power of speech and thought but are chary of locomotion. He intoned, " 'The devil hath not in all his quiver's choice, an arrow for the heart like a sweet voice.' "

Farber's laugh was part of a leer as he winked at Carney. "There's a lady coming in to work for me."

Carney kept his face straight and calm. "Fine. You want to show me the best eatery?"

They walked down Main Street, passing the Wells Fargo station, the feedstore, the Grange Hall. There was a clean restaurant with a painted front. Farber paused and said, "It's run by a good old gal named Madge Margate. She'll take care of you. There's a hotel of sorts across the street, see? Her husband runs it. Tell them you're working for me."

"You and Doc sure have done well here," Carney said.

"We're going to do better. This town will grow into a city someday. We're here first. All we have to do is protect our interests."

"I reckon you can do that," said Carney.

Farber looked sharply at him, and for a moment the good nature, the friendliness was evaporated. "You can bet that across the board, Carney."

"There comes the stage," Carney told him, and stepped inside the restaurant. He lingered there a moment, watching.

He saw Betsy Gaye climb down, a bit wilted from the long journey. He saw Fuller wrestle her carpetbag and her trunk, saw Farber take charge, greeting her bareheaded, all smiles and courtesy. She would be staying at the Margate House, he supposed. He went to the rear of the restaurant and seated himself, back against the wall, facing the doors to the street and to the kitchen. He eased his Colt's around to where it was not unhandy.

A woman stood before him, arms akimbo. She was not old, she was not young. She was, however, used. She had warm brown eyes and red hair beneath a kerchief tied saucily atop her scalp. She wore a checkered apron and a slim skirt.

"Bacon and eggs or hot cakes with molasses," she said. "Or I could cook you a piece of beef."

"Ma'am," he said, grinning at her, "my name's Carney. I could eat just about all of that, but cakes, eggs, and bacon'll do fine."

She returned his smile, went to the kitchen door and said, "Flannels and hen fruit, a rasher of pig for a hungry man."

Then she came back and stood another minute, looking at him. She had laugh wrinkles at the corner of her wide mouth, and her nose was short and slightly snubbed.

"Don't look as if you'd lost anything, at least not to my old eyes," she told him. "I'll bet you're going to work for Cork."

"That's right, ma'am, how'd you guess?"

"I'm a real good guesser. Doc and Cork, they can't depend on old Dan Shriver too much."

"Why should they have to?"

"Remember what Abe Lincoln said? 'You can fool some of the people some of the time . . .' Remember?"

"I remember." He couldn't decide whether she was teasing him or warning him or just making conversation. He did realize that she was not an ordinary woman. "Seems to me a man's better off not tryin' to fool anybody—not unless he can back it up real good."

"You got the point, Will Carney." She winked at him and turned away.

The door opened, and Betsy Gaye came in, closely followed by the attentive Cork Farber. Carney fixed her with a stoney gaze, shaking his head a fraction, looking away as if disinterested. She opened her mouth, closed it again, and let Farber show her to a table up front, near the street door. Mrs. Margate went toward them, and he leaned back, relaxing his muscles but watching everything from the corner of his eye, a trick he had learned long ago in gaming rooms.

Farber had fancy manners, all right, pulling out

49

Betsy's chair, fussing over her, ordering from the lady proprietor in the grand fashion. He had a real limp wrist, Carney noted, like a regular dude. Betsy seemed plain worn out and somewhat puzzled.

He actually was not certain why he had pretended not to know she was on the stage or why he had tipped her to disclaim him. Maybe it was something about Doc Reynolds, the strange way he had of speaking when in drink, his little excursions into poetry, his sliding eyes, which never quite met yours, always seeming fixed on the middle distance. Maybe it was Cork's glibness, his airy assumption that he was the boss and Carney the one who needed favors.

Furthermore, he wondered, how did they know he was in trouble? They had asked the question right off, so they must have had some advance information. News sure had traveled fast. He had ridden Star into the ground to get to Sautelle ahead of the stage, yet he would bet that Reynolds and Farber were more or less expecting him. There was one thing a man on the run had to learn and hold onto—a special understanding of people the way they thought and the way they might act under certain circumstances. Cork and Doc owed him a favor, but they didn't act as though they were returning it. They acted as though they were being generous, as though he needed them a whole lot more than they needed him.

He was not quite sure that this was correct, although he admitted the possibility. If he wanted to stick around, he needed support. The Eggerly clan could reach great distances, possibly as far as Sautelle. He could leave Arizona and go in almost any direction, but if he felt that it was important to be here, he could use help.

It was the girl, of course. He might as well face up to it. In Tombstone it got started somehow. In Tucson she had busted him out of the hoosegow, no question about it. Fuller wouldn't have done it alone. Now he owed her and he had to stay until he saw that she was all right, or at least as well off as a girl on her own in the West could manage.

The kitchen door swung open, and Fuller came into the restaurant. He looked around, saw Carney, and

50

asked a question with his eyes. When he received a nod, he came over and sat down. Betsy was watching them while paying close attention to Farber's easy flow of conversation.

Carney said, "This meal's on me. And thanks."

"It was the gal," Fuller said. "Hell, I never did anything as crazy as that in my life, not when I was sober. How come you and her ain't eatin' outa the same trough tonight?"

A Negro man came from the kitchen bearing Carney's food, which gave him time to think. When it was placed before him and Fuller had given Mrs. Margate his order, he was ready.

He said, "I'm going to work with Cork Farber. It occurred to me the least said about jailbreaking the better. I'd admire if you'd clam up about it."

"You think I want the Eggerlys on my trail? I was hopin' you'd keep quiet about it your own self." He smeared a hot roll liberally with a piece of butter between its halves. Speaking past a mouthful, he went on, "I shouldn't even be settin' here talkin' to you. It was Miss Gaye got me wound up."

"She's doing all right. She's also going to work for Cork Farber."

Fuller swallowed. "And that ain't a good idea. He's got a bad name with women. I done told her, over and over. But she's got some bug about it. Says she wants to make some money offen him before she makes a move."

"What kind of move?"

"I dunno. That's a gal can shut up her mouth when she wants to. Fact of the matter is, she's got ways with her, she can get a man off balance, sorta. I been up and down and all over this country for many a year. You wouldn't believe it, but I was with Kit Carson in the mountains. I was with him at Val Verde durin' the war. Sergeant, I was, and him a Colonel and the Confeds shootin' at us and some damn fool loadin' the mules with dynamite and ruinin' the whole battle when they turned and run our way. Yep, I been there, and I seen women from and includin' the Blackfoot squaws before the pox

51

uglied them up, pretty as speckled hens. I been in Taos with the Spanish gals and in Dodge—but you was in Dodge. In my way I been with a passel of gals. I never did see one like Miss Gaye, so independent and nervy and good-lookin' at that."

Carney said, "Seems like she made a believer of you."

"Only one thing the matter with her."

"What's that?"

"She's purely got a hankerin' for you."

Carney choked a bit of bacon. His weather eye caught Betsy looking at him across the room as Farber talked and talked at her. He swallowed hard.

"That's all blarney," he said. "I was able to do her a small favor, she returned it in Tucson, that's all."

"Favor? Killin' Bud Eggerly is a small favor?"

"I didn't go to kill him," Carney explained. "He was makin a fuss in the Oriental. I hustled him outside. He fired twice at me, and I had to down him."

"Knowin' he was the apple of Simon's eye." Fuller reached for another biscuit. "Kinda reckless, wasn't it? Supposin' he hadn't been pesterin' the gal? Would you of killed him?"

Carney thought for a moment, then said, "Truthful, I don't know. A man pulls a gun, shoots at you a couple times. He's walkin' toward you, he can't keep missing. You do what you have to do. It was dark. I aimed to stop him from getting me. He died. You put a name on it."

"The judge called it self-defense. There was plenty of witnesses. But Simon don't cotton to the decision. You knowed Simon wouldn't."

Carney scarcely heard the stage driver. He was trying to express his creed for the first time, trying to make it clear to himself why he acted as he did. "Sometimes I wonder. A man don't start out to be a gunfighter. Things happen. He's quick or he's dead. Then he gets a name. Then people come at him; people he don't know, don't care about. There's not enough law to stop them. He's got to protect himself. Pretty soon he's on the move. He

52

didn't want it that way to begin with, he hates running. But what's he going to do?"

"Change his name. Get outa the country." Fuller rubbed his nose with a gnarled finger. "I dunno. I feel for you, Carney. You ain't like Hickock or Thompson —or Hardin or them. You ain't got that look in your eye. Maybe it's just your luck is bad. I reckon you'll do somethin' about it. I dunno what. But—excuse me for sayin' so—if a man wants out, he can always find a way."

"Can he?" The urge to talk was gone. Carney ate silently, listening to Fuller ramble on about old gunfights, old trapper fights, old Indian fights. He kept one eye on Betsy Gaye, half hearing, half wondering what the future would bring, unable to take his mind off the girl and her possible relationship with Farber and why she had come here and what her plans might be.

He finished his meal and shoved back his chair. Fuller's tray appeared, and the stage driver waved a hand.

"Go right ahead. I got a lot of catchin' up on my fodder to do."

Mrs. Margate was behind a counter at the front of the place. Carney walked slowly toward her, took out some money. "I want to pay for Fuller, too."

She said, "A cartwheel will do it. Food all right?"

"It was fine," Carney told her. "Real fine. I'll be staying at the hotel."

"Charlie will take care of you." Her face went all hard for a moment, then fell into the humorous lines he had first noted. "Charlie takes care of everybody."

"Just fine," said Carney. He turned toward the door and then heard Farber call his name. He went over to the table, hat in hand.

"This is Miss Betsy Gaye. She'll be working with us," Farber said. "Will Carney, Miss Gaye."

"How do you do? I believe we've seen each other before," she said.

"Tombstone," Carney said, nodding. "I remember."

Farber looked sharply from one to the other, then relaxed, as they seemed merely polite, as acquaintances might be. "Well, get settled in, then come over to the place, Carney. We'll go over the routine."

53

"Okay." Carney nodded to Betsy Gaye and went out onto the street. It was bright and unseasonably warm. He walked back to the tie rack and led Star down the street to the livery stable. He left the horse, gave the man a dollar, shouldered his bedroll, and carried his saddle-bag to the hotel. It was quite new, unpainted, two stories high, a modest enough building. He went into a small lobby. Behind the desk a man sat in an armchair of rawhide softened with cushions and beamed at him.

Charlie Margate was completely bald. His shoulders were as wide as a barn. He had arms like a gorilla, one of which he raised in greeting. When he smiled, it was as if a graveyard opened a row of tombstones to the public view. He said, "Carney, welcome to Margate House."

"News gets around fast." He dropped his gear and put both hands on the counter. He saw then why Charlie Margate did not rise.

The big man sat in a bucket chair on wheels. His legs were covered by a Navajo blanket. There was a special low desk at his hand, with ledger, guest book, pen, and ink. He lifted the register and proffered it.

"Sautelle's a small burg, and people know I can't get around. They tell me things." The smile flashed again. There was only surface humor in it.

Carney signed his name. "If I could have some hot water, I'd appreciate it. It's been a long haul."

"So I hear. What about that Apache medicine man? You get any news of him?"

"Nok-e-da-klinne?"

"The one that's stirrin' them up," said Margate. "Nobody believes he can make trouble. A man like me—half a man, that is—maybe he thinks more about an Indian raid. Sautelle's too soft to stand up under any real trouble. Maybe that's why you're staying?"

"I sure don't intend to fight an Indian war all by my own self," said Carney. "Yes, Fireboy is out. And he's dangerous. You can pass that along to whoever's interested besides yourself."

"I'll do just that." Now Margate was serious, his brow wrinkling. His eyebrows were colorless, which

54

seemed to dehumanize him. "Four dollars a week all right?"

"Here's a week in advance." Carney put the money down.

"Here's a key to Room Four. Top of the stairs, over the street. It won't be noisy by the time you go to bed." Margate raised his voice. "Milton! Water for Mr. Carney."

A dull-faced young man, possibly twenty, came and gaped, then vanished toward the rear. Carney gathered his belongings and went up the stairs. Margate was an odd one, he thought. Puts on a good face, but he hates being crippled, hates his wife working the restaurant, fears Indians and probably a lot of other things. The frontier was a hard place on cripples, even a quiet town like Sautelle. The man was right, too—the Apaches were not much for raiding towns, but a setup like this might appeal to a crazy medicine man like Nok-e-da-klinne. If he made a successful foray here, as the military would say, he might get the rest of the White Mountain tribe to pay attention to him. It was the kind of coup that might be just the thing for him.

He went into Room 4 and found it large, with two windows, a wide bed with a gay coverlet, a washstand with a huge crockery basin and a pitcher, over which was a mirror, not too murky. It was all rather new and had not been beat up by too many wild nights. He unpacked his small wardrobe, hanging up a black gambler's coat and striped pants, unwrapping town boots of soft leather, stowing his clean shirts in a low bureau.

He stripped down to his underwear, then took out his Colt's and examined it with great care. He revolved the cylinder, broke and emptied it, eased the hammer back, and let it down gently, making certain no speck of dust had clung to it. He took out a tiny oilcan and a rag and ramrod and cleansed the barrel. He put it back into firing order just as there was a knock on the door. He held onto the gun, saying, "Come in."

Milton, the half-witted boy, entered carrying a steaming pail of water. When he saw the gun in Carney's hand, he gaped, frozen in his tracks, stammering syllables that did not make sense.

55

Carney put down the revolver, got up slowly, and took the steaming pail from flaccid hands. "Son, nobody's going to hurt you."

Milton said, "Y-Y-You . . . y-y-you . . . y-y-you're Carney!"

"Yes, but I don't go around shooting boys. Or even grown men, for that matter."

Milton gasped, "Y-Y-You've killed people!"

"That's a fact, and now can I take a wash before the water gets cold?"

A gleam came into the pale, vacant eyes. Milton said, "G-G-G-Gee, I got somebody I wish I could kill."

He turned and ran. Carney closed the door, lifted the pail, and poured water into the bowl. When he had finished, he stared at himself in the mirror.

"Yeah," he said to his reflection. "And I bet everybody, down deep, has got somebody he'd like to kill."

The idea gave him some small comfort as he washed himself from head to toe. He put on clean underwear of a light woven texture. He found a can of talcum and sprinkled it on his body—that was a trick he had learned from a woman in Denver. The odor was pleasant. He stretched himself on the bed, conscious of weariness. He reached for the Colt's, placed it on a low table near his hand and relaxed.

His mind went over various matters, refusing him sleep, although a nap would have been welcome. He thought of the hard ride from Tucson, of nearly running onto the Apache ritual dance, thus finishing his career alone in the dark and none the wiser.

Excepting the girl, he thought, she'd have missed him. She certainly must have believed he would show here in Sautelle. He wondered what she had meant when she told Fuller that she would "make a move." In what direction? What was it that sent her to this place from Tombstone? He really did not know her very well, they had exchanged no confidences, but she had been mighty particular about telling him her destination.

And Farber, what about him? In Denver he had been the underdog, and it was right to side him and snake him out of the setup. Doc Reynolds had been only a by-

56

stander, a friend of Farber's, so far as Carney knew. Now they were close partners and they seemed to have Sautelle where the hair is short.

Farber and the girl, he thought, there is something between them, maybe something one of them don't know about. It will make for fireworks, he'd bet. Betsy Gaye attracts action, as with Bud Eggerly, maybe always the wrong kind of action, the trouble kind.

Well, he owed her, and that was that. If it didn't go any further, at least he had to try and repay her. What he did, chousing Bud Eggerly, was what any man might do. What she did, breaking him out of that jail, that was extra special. They would have murdered him in cold blood if she had left him in there. He couldn't pass up a favor like that.

Then there was that restaurant woman, Mrs. Margate. The way she had looked at him was another matter. And the manner in which she had spoken of her husband, not what she said, the tone of her voice, and him crippled at the hips and tied to a chair. She wasn't a bad-looking woman, either, nothing like the drudges he had seen in western towns cooking over hot stoves to feed the public. She had help in the kitchen, she was making it pretty good, he reckoned. And the hotel, too, it must pay enough to provide them with free rent. He wondered where they lived in the hotel, how she managed with him, the poor man, dressing him and all that.

She was, in her way, a mighty fine looking woman. Carney's eyes half closed, he began to drift off into sleep. Betsy Gaye was better looking and younger—and unspoiled, too.

There was a tap at his door, almost a scratch, like a kitten would make. He leaped out of bed, grabbing his revolver. He stood aside from the door and unbolted it. He said, "Come in slow and easy."

The door opened with a snap, and Betsy leaped inside and closed it behind her. Then she leaned hard against it.

He grabbed for clothing, saying, "My Gawd, gal, you can't come in here like this."

"I'm already in," she whispered. "Don't get all

wrought up, I've seen men in their underwear before."

Even as he struggled into his pants he showed shock, goggling at her.

She snickered. "Don't be like the others, Will. Remember, I worked at Nell Cashman's making beds. Those miners were up and down all hours."

He said, "I didn't say anything. I mean, well a gal could have brothers. Anything a-tall."

"No brothers," she said. "Nor uncles nor cousins nor aunts. Are you all right now?"

He yanked a shirt on over his head, found sox, and pulled them on. "What's got into you, anyway?"

She crossed the room and, standing carefully aside, pulled down the shade, went to the other window and did the same. Then she perched on the edge of his bed. "They do run a clean place. That's a relief. Mr. Margate's a something, isn't he? The way he looked me up and down!"

Carney said, "Is that why you come in here, to talk about the town?"

"Partly," she agreed. "And partly about Cork Farber."

"Uh-huh." He had fully recovered himself, he was interested. "What about friend Farber?"

"It was clever of you not to recognize me in the restaurant. That Mrs. Margate's got eyes like a hawk."

"What's she got to do with it?"

"You never can tell, a red-headed woman with a crippled husband," said Betsy somewhat vaguely. "Anyway, it's best they don't know about us."

"There's not much to know excepting you saved my life in Tucson," said Carney. "I owe you for that."

"Yes, you do. I mean, you're welcome and all, but I want you on my side."

"You've got a side?"

She said, "Will, do you remember Macie Grant?"

He thought for a moment. "A little dark girl. Kind of quiet? Played piano?"

"A very nice girl. She was my good friend."

58

"I think I knew her. Minded her own business, didn't drink nor work the men."

"That was Macie. Just before things went bad in Tombstone, I had a letter from her. Here—read it." She produced a much-folded piece of paper from her reticule.

Carney moved toward the window but did not raise the shade, using a crack of light at its edge.

Dear Betsy:
The job is all right, Sautelle is fine. The cowboys are about the same as Tombstone, but otherwise it is much quieter and nicer. Cork Farber is fine. He is very nice to me. Doc Reynolds, his partner, is a cold fish, but Cork is very nice to me and kind.

I hope things are all right with you. I would like very much to see you. If you can make a trip, please come up on the stage. Cork would like you. He's very hansum. I hope you can make it up here.

Hugs and Kisses,
Macie

P.S. Cork is taking me for a buggy ride to-night. Isn't that thrilling?
M.

Betsy handed over a clipping from the Tombstone *Epitaph.* "Now read this."

Carney looked at the newsprint. *Local Girl Dies . . . Macie Grant, formerly of Tombstone, passed away in Sautelle, this paper learned yesterday. She was riding in a buggy when the horse bolted and threw her among rocks, which fractured her skull. Too bad, she was a good un.*

"That is too bad," said Carney. "I'm right sorry."

"Yes. So am I. Specially since Macie wasn't thrown out of any buggy because the horse ran away."

"How do you know that?"

"Because she was deathly afraid of horses and wouldn't hold a rein to keep herself alive. She wouldn't ride in a buggy alone for a million dollars. It was like

59

a sickness, the way she feared horses. Unless she was forced or was very much in love, she wouldn't get that near one."

"I don't see what you're driving at," Carney said, although he thought he was beginning to catch the idea, and it was one he did not like to think about.

She seemed to sense his discomfort. Her eyes grew larger, she looked at him earnestly, saying, "Will, let me tell you something about women. They understand each other as no man can believe. They can't fool one another. You thought I was being mean about Mrs. Margate, didn't you? Well, I saw her look at you and I saw her eye me and Farber. I know as much as I want to know about her. Macie Grant and I were like sisters. In that town there weren't many of us unmarried who didn't . . . didn't . . . you know." She flushed to her hair roots.

He said gently, "I know, Betsy."

"Thanks." She took the clippings and the letter from him and tore them to bits as she went on. "Macie was in love with Farber. I know that for real sure. But when I asked about her, he said she was a poor, unlucky girl. The way he said it, he was lying. He was trying to change the subject. His eyes flickered, he was upset. There was something very wrong about Macie's death. I'm going to find out the truth, and if it's what I think it was, I'm going to send Farber to the gallows."

Carney drew a deep breath, exhaled. "Betsy, you've got to be loco."

"Macie was dear to me. She didn't deserve to be hurt."

Carney said, "Why, sure. That's fine. But she's been dead some time, you see. And this town is run by Cork and Doc. The law is their law. It's a cinch nobody saw what happened. How you goin' to find out anything?"

"I couldn't excepting you're here."

He said, "Now, wait a minute. Farber's supposed to be my friend. I'm working for him."

"What if he killed her?"

"You couldn't prove it nohow." But he felt suddenly uncomfortable.

60

She said, "I asked about Cork Farber. I found out he has a bad reputation with women."

"Who did you ask?"

"Wyatt Earp," she told him.

"You asked Wyatt?"

"I certainly did. He knew Farber in Dodge City. He told me the man is no good where women are concerned. I'll tell you the truth, Will. Wyatt was going to look into it for me, just before Morgan Earp got killed and all the trouble began."

He said, "I'll be dogged."

"Look at it another way," she pressed on. "Supposing I'm wrong? Then, it would be awful to suspect Farber, wouldn't it? Now that you know about Macie, and I know about her, it would be bad to suspect him. All I want's the truth."

"You didn't tell me any of this in Tombstone."

"Why should I? You didn't owe me anything."

"Yeah," he said. "I can see that." She was a very pretty girl in this light. She had a lot of nerve. He said, half to himself, "No matter where I go, it's complicated. One way or another."

"Everything is complicated," she told him, and for a moment she looked too young and somewhat frightened.

He hastened to reassure her. "I'll think about it. If Farber killed the gal, he ought to pay for it. Play it the way we started, make believe you don't know me too well."

"As long as you're on my side." She drew a deep breath of relief and was alive again, vital, confident. "Thank you, Will."

"You better get out of here now." He opened his door and looked up and down the hall. No one was in view.

For a moment she was very close to him. She wrinkled her nose, leaned against him, sniffing. In his ear she said softly, "My, you smell nice, for a man."

He gave her a small shove, and she fled across to the door of Number 6. He watched in both directions as she inserted her key, opened the door, stepped inside the

61

room. As he retreated into Number 4 she blew him a kiss.

He bolted himself in, sat down on the bed, and tried to think with some clarity. It seemed to come down to what he had said earlier to the girl, that no matter where he went, there was something to put him on the run.

Chapter Six

THE AFTERNOON SUN cooled off, the air was brisk. Carney slept in his room at the Margate House, his hand outstretched toward his gun.

Below stairs Mrs. Margate stood hipshot, one hand on the desk, looking down at her husband. He was rolling a cigarette in brown paper, his hands strong and pliable and sure.

"I wouldn't fool around with him," he said.

"Dear Charlie. Smiling Charlie," she responded.

"He's not your kind. He's hard, like rock. And he's unlucky."

She said, "But a man, now, isn't he? A real man."

He stuck the cigarette into the corner of his large mouth and struck a match, cupping his hands, blowing smoke. "Not referring to my condition, as I well know."

"Have I ever?"

"No. That you have spared me. The world thinks of you as a good and patient wife. The world is right . . . almost."

"I've never deceived you, Charlie."

"You never lied to me," he corrected her.

"When I do, that'll be the end."

He put his hands on the chair arms. In one lifting motion he raised his body without effort. He hung there like a side of beef, his legs dangling, useless, swaying on those powerful arms, looking at her.

"Yes," she said. "Yes, I know you'd strangle me if you made up your mind. I live with that knowledge.

That's all you ever had, Charlie, that strength in your muscles. You never had much in your heart."

She turned and went to the stairs. He dropped back into the rawhide chair. His pillows were disarranged. He straightened them with deft shifting of his torso.

He called, "You won't get anywhere with him, Madge."

She did not answer. She climbed the stairs and went into Room 8 at the end of the hall. She took off the dress that smelled like cooked food and let down her hair and sat before a mirror, picking up a brush, stroking her auburn locks, slowly, steadily. She paused to spray cologne upon the brush, then began again. She was not, she knew, regarding her reflection, a beautiful woman, but she could think like one and sometimes delude herself—and others. She thought about Cork Farber and trembled as the anger brought color to her cheeks. Her hand holding the brush began to shake. and she stopped its motion, sitting, staring, facing her humiliation, trying not to deceive herself.

It was a daily ritual. It kept her going, an honest attempt to brook the truth, to admit defeat. She accepted shame, the unsteadiness of her hands in order to gain strength by acknowledging the truth. And maybe, just maybe, someday she could find a way to kill Cork Farber.

In a moment she could pick up her brush and proceed with her toilette. In a little while she put on a heavier dress, formfitting, flaring at the bottom of the skirt, against the chill that would increase through the afternoon and night. Farber had discarded her for Macie Grant, and that was a fact. She would face facts.

It was true that she did not lie to her husband, but neither did she proffer the truth. If he knew—and he learned a lot through the gossip of Dan Shriver and the mutterings of Milton, before whom anyone would talk—Charlie refused to admit it to himself, much less to her. His specialty was innuendo, it had always been that way. There was no stability in his character. There never had been, back in Chicago, when his cowardice had trapped them in a burning building from which he had finally

63

jumped to save his life and ruin both his legs. Another man had carried her to safety on that occasion.

The knowledge of her ability to attract and use men —now admittedly somewhat in the sere—gave her the strength to leave the room and walk down the hall. She paused between Rooms 4 and 6, shrugged, went on. Charlie was still behind the desk, reading a book. They looked at one another in passive hostility, then she crossed the street.

In front of the restaurant a small, blanketed Indian shuffled past her. She thought she caught a glimpse of fanatical, shining, threatening eyes, then the dark face was averted as he continued up toward the Cowboy Saloon. Cork and Doc were seated on the verandah, each with a drink. Madge Margate waved to Mrs. Dan Shriver, who was coming from the general store, and went into the restaurant.

Mrs. Dan Shriver wagged a greeting and kept going down 2nd Street to the square, unlovely cottage that was her home. She was a small woman, with a large nose, which had all her life been an embarrassment. She would not have been bad-looking had she not inherited the Eggerly nose, she always believed.

Actually she was not in any way a handsome woman. Her chin was too strong and long, her ears were set low on her skull, which was egg-shaped. Her hair was not heavy enough to cover the bony outline of this odd head, and her large, dark eyes were too close together.

The kitchen was the biggest room in the house and the best equipped. Sally Shriver, a nearsighted, plump child of eleven, was attending to Dan Jr., who was a baby. Ma Shriver—her name was Marylin, but the family always called her "Ma," which she hated—put down her bundle and picked up the boy child.

Sally said, "I think he's hungry. He's been bawlin' his head off."

In Ma's arms the baby seemed contented. He goggled at her and drooled a little. She wiped his mouth. He already had a nose too big for his face and a heavy jaw.

"All Eggerly," she said proudly.

"That's a damn lie," growled Dan Shriver. He appeared in the bedroom door, rumpled from his siesta. He went to the kitchen sink and worked the pump handle, laving his pouting face with cold water, rinsing his hands as though to wash away invisible stains.

"The nose, the chin, strong," proclaimed Ma. "Them's Eggerly features, man."

Sally whined, "I'm goin' over to Leedses house and play with Linda."

"You're goin' to do chores," said Ma sternly.

"Let her go," said Dan. "Leeds is an important man. Let her mingle with Linda."

Sally, who had the pink skin and inclination to avoirdupois of the Shrivers, winked at her father and departed.

Ma said, "You and the important people. No Eggerly needs to think about who's who, not anyplace."

He went to the cooling box outside the window and found a loaf of oven-cooked bread and a half pound of yellow cheese. He sat at the table with a large slicing knife and began to eat. She sat opposite him, holding the baby, waiting, knowing he had sent the girl away because she wished to speak with her.

He said, "You'll get a chance to talk with your Eggerly clan. I sent for them."

"Don't see no other way." She had heard the whole of his dilemma as soon as he could get to her and tell her of it. "If they found out, and you didn't tell them, then it'd really be bad."

"No, I hadda tell 'em." He ate bread and cheese. "They got to leave Carney alone until I give 'em the word."

"They don't like to be told," she warned him.

He cut a hunk of the cheese, held it impaled on the point of the blade, shaking it at her. "Ma, you got to get things in y'all's head and get 'em straight. Simon is big down south. Farber is just as big up here. My job and your livin' depends on Farber. You unnastand that?"

"No Eggerly is a fool." She sat bolt upright, the child nestling close to her. "What I meant is, I can talk to 'em better than you. I know you ain't as dumb as some people think. I know you got sand enough when it comes to a pinch. I'm your wife and I ain't ashamed of you."

He lowered the knife to the table and slowly pried off the piece of cheese. "Ma, I don't mean to be ugly. I got me a peck of trouble."

"You have," she said, nodding. "It ain't your makin', neither. We're town folk, you and me, we never did want to grub in the earth nor chase cows. You got a good enough job, the way you work it. We got a nice piece of money stored in that chimney. We get a little more, we go down to Simon and show him, and he'll give us our due."

"I'd jest as soon go back to Alabama," he said.

"And leave the Eggerlys?"

"Well, now." He thought a moment. "No, you're right. Only like it is now, I can't do nothin' about Carney, and Simon ain't goin' to like it."

"You can't do nothing about him right now," she amended. "Now ain't tomorrow or next day. You let me talk to the boys. You can keep an eye on Carney, can't you?"

"I keep an eye on a lot of things hereabouts."

"You do. So we're layin' low and when it's safe and easy, we'll do what's to be done," she said briskly. She got up and put the baby in a cradle, which rocked gently under the table. "I better redd up and arrange some fixins for the boys. You let me handle 'em, Dan."

He sighed with relief. "Yeah, Ma. You handle 'em."

She went out in the yard and looked toward the Leeds house up the street, a much larger one than hers. The owners of the general store did not have a poke as big as the one Dan had gouged from the town, she would bet. She went into the hen house and found seven eggs. She came out with them in her apron. There were three Eggerlys nearby and three cousins down among the ranches. Bo, Peter, and Jack would be coming in, they represented the family in such a situation. She had a dozen eggs in the house and plenty of side meat and grits. She'd make an omelette, she decided. She looked off toward the mountains and saw an Indian walking swiftly, toeing

66

in, removing a blanket from his shoulders. He was an Apache by his headband, and she wondered, since Apaches were not blanket Indians, as a rule. He vanished into the mesquite that edged the end of the street where Sautelle petered out, and a moment later she saw him going up the slope among the piñon trees astride a paint pony.

She shook her head, but it seemed unimportant. She had to think about what she was going to do for the Eggerly brothers, who loved to eat even as they conferred.

On the verandah of the Cowboy Saloon the two men sipped their drinks at their leisure. Doc had hit his alcoholic plateau for the day and was neither drunk nor sober. Farber looked down Main Street, now beginning to come alive as the day waned and people shopped for supper or began wandering toward his saloon. Two miners crossed and went past him and inside.

" 'My only books are woman's looks, and folly's all they taught me,' " quoted Doc. "On the other hand, she's a lovely piece, Betsy Gaye."

"I've told you often enough, lay off," Farber said.

"Oh, yes, I forgot." Doc laughed. "And the Eggerlys are coming to town, tra-la, the enemy's coming to town."

"Not our enemies. Not yet," said Farber. "Too many of them. If there was only some way we could get Carney in a jackpot and then see to it that he eliminated a few of them, that would be a fine happenstance."

"They won't try him, not this time."

"No, they won't, because Ma Shriver will talk them out of it. I wonder if Carney's sleeping?"

"I wonder if the girl's sleeping. She and Carney in the same hotel, rooms opposite each other. Charlie Margate's thoughtful that way. Better Betsy than Madge, eh?"

Farber reddened. "I keep telling you, Doc. Lay off."

"It's for your own good. You have to keep cool about women, Cork." Reynolds was persuasive, soothing in his tone. "Have your fun but be more prudent. You're not a miner nor a gambler nor a drover, you're

67

an important man and you'll be more important. I'm only trying to keep you on the path to better things."

"I know, Doc, I know." He finished his drink. "I have to admit you're right."

A dog broke shrilly from the alley next to the livery stable, and four boys ran in pursuit. Behind them lumbered Milton, from the hotel. Ed Leeds came out and chased them away from his store. Reverend Peterson strolled past the saloon, bowing with dignity, an old man with a lined face. Will Carney came from Margate House and began walking toward the Cowboy Saloon.

Doc said, "It is best to let him know there are Eggerlys in the county, I believe."

"Not yet. We may need him."

"He won't run."

"It's not that. I want him free and easy. Then if anything happens, he'll stick with us all the way."

"You're thinking about the girl, not Carney," Doc warned him. "There's nothing pressing right now. You're obsessed with the idea of having the quick gun around as protection. Against what?"

"I have a hunch," said Farber. "I have a strong feeling that Carney is important to us."

"Logic is against it."

"I don't care about logic when I get this feeling."

Doc drained his glass and arose. "I know better than to argue the point. I'm going down and get a hot meal."

Farber said, "And another thing. You're always lecturing me about women. Better you didn't give Madge that ugly grin. She's not like a lot of other women. Lay off her, too."

Doc said, "Listen to the mockingbird!" He laughed and went down the steps.

Carney met him halfway. They paused and exchanged greetings.

Doc asked, "Everything all right at the hotel?"

"Just fine. Had a nap."

"Good. Did you run into the new girl entertainer?"

"No such luck. Mighty handsome gal."

"That's what Farber thinks."

"He's got good taste. Well, see you later?"

68

"Indeed," said Doc. "Unless Mrs. Leeds decides to deliver the brat tonight. Takes her hours, sometimes days. And she's about due. So long, Carney."

He went down the street, wondering what it would be like to wear a gun and have people fear you and still remain clear-eyed and sober and almost like other folks.

Almost, but not quite, he added, there was that something in Carney, a watchfulness, a tension. It took a strong man to carry that around. He shivered in the cool evening air, making for the restaurant.

Chapter Seven

CARNEY STOOD AT the end of the long bar of the Cowboy Saloon and was impressed. People had begun to fill the place as the supper hour ended. Everything was immaculate. He had not noticed the chandeliers before, huge wagon wheels from long-gone Conestogas, hung in heavy chains and supporting coal lamps with circular wicks that gave off illumination as bright as day. The pictures on the walls were not nude women but landscapes, paintings of mountain and desert, a portrait of a Sioux chieftain in full panoply.

"Sure beats the Long Branch in Dodge," he said.

"You got to give Doc credit for that," said Farber. "He builds for the future. And the crowd will grow because of the new entertainer."

The long bar was polished, the scar-faced bartender had two neatly dressed Mexican helpers. An old swamper kept the cuspidors cleansed. There was sawdust on the floor around the feet of the men at the mahogany. Voices were a polite hum. Several times Carney caught quick glances from slitted eyes and knew they were talking about him, resenting him. He was accustomed to such reaction in new places, it did not perturb him.

The piano in the corner sat upon a small platform.

69

The gaming tables were removed from it by service tables and chairs, at which several men had taken early places.

Farber said, "Come on, take a look around. Doc's got a lot of original ideas."

There was a room set apart, not too large but adequate, behind hanging strings of beads, which formed a portiere. There were lamps in wall brackets, discreetly low. The tables were smaller and the chairs more comfortable.

"The ladies' parlor," said Farber proudly. "Also for people like D. Brand, the banker, who brings his wife sometimes. They can enjoy the entertainment without being bothered."

"It's a nice, clean place," said Carney.

"Doc's idea, exactly. He says when the law comes, we'll be so decent that we'll have time to look around, go into something big."

"Never saw anything like it," Carney admitted.

"Now you see why we can't afford trouble. That's part of your job."

"Yeah, I see." There were stairs leading up to the apartments where Doc and Farber dwelt, but he was not asked to inspect them. He went back into the bar. It was almost time for Betsy Gaye to make her appearance. He had not known that she could entertain, at the Oriental she had served drinks and danced with the patrons. He was aware of anxiety for fear she would not be capable of holding this crowd or that she'd get frightened and be unable to go on at all.

The people kept coming. Ed Leeds went into the parlor to join his wife and the banker. They were starchily dressed people, dull as dishwater, Carney had seen many of their kind and knew that Doc Reynolds was right, these were the future citizens of the West. Settled country depended upon such as they, the government of the towns must be theirs, they came into the frontier after it was made safe by the mountain men and the gunslinging marshals and the troops and made it theirs. It was the way things had to be. There could be no future without children, and Carney and his kind were not ones to settle down with families, he thought.

Marshal Dan Shriver came in, his face shiny with soap, his eyes squinting at Carney, sliding off, going around. He found a place against the wall in the rear, between the parlor and the dais. It seemed that everyone was here to get a first look at the new girl, which was a tribute to Farber and Reynolds. Carney's thoughts went to Macie Grant, who had been a fine pianist, he remembered dimly. She must have been popular here for the town to have such curiosity about her successor.

Farber was mixing with the customers. Every so often he bought a drink for a favored few. He was a handsome young man, all right. Macie had spelled it "hansum."

Carney was restless. If Betsy were right, Farber was a killer, or at least a despoiler of women. Wyatt had known the man, had been willing to check up on him. It was a hard thing to believe about someone you knew.

Doc Reynolds came in the front door, his face glum, hat brim pulled low. He did not respond to greetings, making a beeline for the stairs leading upward. Farber intercepted him, and Carney thought he saw the marks of five fingers on Doc's right cheek. The partners talked in low tones for a moment, then Reynolds flung away and went upstairs, Farber staring after him, angry but speechless. Carney's unrest increased.

The crowd had settled down now, and it was interesting to see the pecking order. Carney's eye could pick out each distinct group, the miners nearest the door and farthest from the dais where Betsy would appear, the cowboys and working men next, then the solid, or nearly solid, merchants and clerks. The end of the bar where he stood was reserved, evidently, for Farber and his guests and for Carney, of course, because it was a vantage point from which the entire scene could be kept under surveillance. The three barkeeps were busy serving, mainly beer for this occasion.

Farber came and stood beside him, and Carney asked, "Who's minding the store?"

"I don't understand." Farber was slightly flushed— a bit upset, it appeared.

"I keep telling you about Nok-e-da-klinne and his

crowd. Also there's a bank and the hotel, and a fire would start a real riot."

Farber said, "Nothing like that happens here. Don't worry about it."

"Just the same, Shriver should be making his rounds," Carney insisted.

"Don't fret yourself." Farber caught a glimpse of a door opening alongside the ladies' parlor and darted toward it. This, Carney thought, must be the dressing room or whatever, because Betsy now came out, and Farber took her by the hand, and silence gradually fell upon the room.

She was wearing a low-cut gown of pure white. Her hair was piled on her head, the light catching the glints of red and putting a sheen upon her. She had a lace scarf around her shoulders and she had fastened a Mexican silken band with tassels about her slender middle. She was a striking figure and suddenly a horny-handed miner clapped his hands together like pistol shots and in a moment everyone had joined him, applauding every step of her way to the piano.

She would do, Carney thought. She had whatever it took. No matter if she was off-key or didn't know the words, the crowd was with her. He finished the small whiskey he had allowed himself and settled against the wall to watch and listen.

Betsy Gaye bowed and bowed, her face alive with pleasure. She stood alongside the piano then and waited. Farber stepped up beside her and held out his hands.

"Ladies and gentlemen of Sautelle, you are most generous in applauding this young lady. Her name is Miss Betsy Gaye, and she will now entertain you."

It was neat but not gaudy, Carney thought, as Farber came down and made his way back to the end of the bar. Betsy moved to the chair, arranged her long skirt, sat down, and turned a wide smile upon the audience.

"Class," whispered Farber. "She's got class."

"Oh, sure," Carney said. "But can she sing?"

Farber looked startled. "Why, of course. You must have heard her in Tombstone."

"Never had the pleasure," Carney lied. He was beginning to get a kick out of this. Betsy looked so smug up there, it would be a real joke if she had no voice and couldn't tinkle the ivories.

She raised her strong white arms, dropped her hands, and fingered the keys. The sound was tinkling but musical. She played a few bars of some soft tune, then the tempo changed. It quickened and became rollicking, and she was singing, "Buffalo gals, won't you come out tonight, come out tonight, come out tonight, buffalo gals won't you come out tonight, by the light of the silv-ry moon."

The Cowboy Saloon began to rock. Men were stamping their feet, joining in their voices. Farber started to protest, but Carney held him back.

"She's got 'em going. Let her," he said. "Smartest thing is to get 'em on her side."

Farber said, "By damn, maybe you're right."

She finished and paused, and again they clapped and now some of them whistled. She looked over their heads at Carney and closed one eye. She did not have a remarkable voice, but she had learned the harpischord back in East Texas and the piano under Macie Grant. She could rouse them and now she sang "Jeannie With The Light Brown Hair," and they were silent, listening to every word, which she articulated with care and feeling.

She was on the second chorus when there was a slight rumpus near the street door. Carney shoved his way through the crowd along the bar as voices rose. A man swore at him as he stepped on a foot, but Carney merely apologized and went on, the foreboding returning in greater strength.

He heard Milton stammer, "G-G-Got to see Carney."

The miners were shoving the boy around, angry, rough. Carney shouldered one of them aside. They were a stocky, bulky breed, powerful as oxen. He snatched Milton loose from their grasp and nudged him toward the door. They lowered their heads and glowered, but Carney smiled, put a finger to his lips, and indicated the stage,

73

where Betsy Gaye had not lost a note of the tender song. Then he followed Milton out onto the wide verandah.

"M-M-Mrs. Margate," the boy was stammering. He saw the hooded, muffled figure halfway down the silent, deserted street then and began to run.

She said, "Something's wrong. Charlie smelled it, Charlie's odd that way sometimes. It's over at Shriver's house behind the hotel there. And it's too quiet. You can hear the quiet."

Carney stood perfectly still for a moment. He could hear the boy breathing behind him, he could feel the beat of his own heart. He thought he heard a far, quickly stifled scream. His hand went to the butt of his gun.

He said "Milton, you've got to get back in there. Go in the ladies' entrance. Tell Farber to get out here with Shriver and as many men as he can, right now. Tell him I said so. But don't yell, don't make any fuss." He turned to the woman. "You go with him."

"No."

"You can't do anything to help. Go with him."

She was already running, awkward, hampered by her skirts, toward the hotel. "No," she said.

He went past her. He kept to the shadows but raced as swiftly as he could to the hotel, down the alley alongside it to the rear of the building. He saw the first sliver of fire. He crouched behind a fence and kept moving. He had only his six-gun and a light belt of ammunition. He came to a clump of weeds and lay in it, shuddering as he thought of the small voice he had heard. The Shriver house was now enveloped in flames. A figure came dodging out, carrying a burning brand.

He took careful aim and fired. Then he moved his position along the flimsy fence as the Apache fell, the torch going into the street, flaming high. Another small, agile Indian tried to stop his forward progress, ranging around with a rifle in his hands. Carney dropped him and threw himself flat on the ground.

A volley of shots echoed on 2nd Street. The house began to burn in earnest, throwing long shadows. A keening voice gave commands in the Apache tongue. Three of them rushed toward the fence.

74

Carney took his time. He cut one off with a bullet in his head, gut-shot the second. The final shot he threw as he began to run and he knew he missed. He flipped open the Colt's and emptied it, zigging and zagging. He rounded the corner of the hotel and dropped into deep shadows, yanking out cartridges, slamming them into place.

They came, half a dozen of them, as though they could, like cats, see in the dark. Carney slapped the last charge home and lay still, knowing they could not see him. He had six chambers loaded now. After that it would be over. He steadied the barrel with his left hand.

There was a booming sound from a window of the hotel. The leading Apache jumped high in the air and fell. Carney shot the second.

A dozen more of them were whooping into action. Carney fired into their midst. They began to retreat, carrying their wounded and dead, as they always did. Carney knelt, knowing better than to pursue. If they ran, it was for the best. He had counted well for what he knew had happened to whoever was in the Shriver house.

There was a booming from Main Street. Carney came to his feet and ran to the rear of the hotel. The Apaches were streaming back down 2nd Street, pausing now and then to return the fire of Cork Farber and Dan Shriver and a few others of the town. Carney whipped in three more shots and saw a buck trip and go ploughing forward on his face, throwing a small bundle from him.

The ponies were close at hand, because they all made flying mounts excepting those carrying their fallen mates. They were gone as though by magic, and Carney turned to shout for water.

There was already a brigade handing buckets to one another. It ran from the hotel and across to the restaurant. He saw Mrs. Margate in the hotel window and went close and looked up at her.

"Nice shootin'," he said.

"I was too late."

"Too late for the beginning. But you saved the town from being burned out."

"Mrs. Shriver and her daughter," she said. Her face

75

was very white. "Charlie kept saying there was something wrong. I saw one of them today on the street. We should have been ready for them."

Carney said, "The poor fellow paid a horrible price."

"That's his house, all right." She leaned out, and he saw the heavy Sharp's rifle in her hands. "I'll have to help Charlie. I knew you'd come through, Carney."

"Thanks again," he said. He went toward the fire line. Farber was organizing a second brigade. Dan Shriver was standing against the hotel wall, his face shriveled, his eyes vacant and lost. Carney paused.

"I haven't got the nerve to go down there," Shriver croaked. "That you, Carney? You got here first. Was —was the fire already started when you got here?"

"I'm real sorry," Carney said.

Shriver pressed both hands against the wall. "She said she saw one of them. She told me, and I paid no heed."

There was nothing to say. Carney stood at the marshal's side. Farber came to them and wiped his brow with a silken kerchief.

"That's what Milton wanted, huh?"

"Mrs. Margate sent him."

Farber looked startled, then sullen. "Guess she saved our bacon. How many'd you get?"

"Half dozen. I had cover, they ran out like quail. We'll never know, they took most of 'em away."

Farber said, "Shriver, I'm sorry. We should've kept a watch."

The marshal groaned, "It was me. I wasn't makin' my rounds."

"They'd have waited until you were at the other end of town," Carney told him. "One man couldn't have stopped them."

"I coulda died," said Shriver. "I could've died with 'em."

"Better take him over to the restaurant," Farber suggested. "They just about got the fire under control."

Shriver said, "No. God knows I don't want to, but I'm goin' down there. I got to go down there."

Carney walked beside him. The marshal seemed to

76

have lost all dimension, as though he were a cardboard figure shambling along in the weird semilight. Enough flame flickered from the brush to allow them to see the blackened house. A huddled figure lay in the street, the last Apache Carney had dropped. Farber walked cautiously toward it, drawing his revolver. The Indian stirred, and Farber shot him twice in the head.

Carney did not flinch, he knew what to expect at the Shriver house. Men stood about, their heads bowed, Farber walked among them and looked down at the two bodies that lay side by side.

Shriver shook like an aspen. A timber flamed up, and the woman and her daughter were briefly outlined, charred, neither distinguishable from the other. The marshal turned blindly away, and Reverend Peterson took charge of him, leading him from the scene.

Farber came to where Carney stood and said, "Had they not stopped for this, they'd have taken the town."

"If it wasn't for the Margates, they'd have burnt it out," Carney told him. "They suspicioned something."

"Why didn't they ring the fire bell, then?"

"They weren't sure." Carney shrugged. "If they were wrong, there'd have been a riot for fair."

"They should have raised the town." Farber scowled. "There's going to be hell to pay when the . . . when her brothers find out what happened."

"Whose brothers?"

"Mrs. Shriver's, that's who." Farber broke off. "We better do something about cleaning up."

"Where's Doc Reynolds? He might be needed."

"Doc is dead drunk by now. You can depend on it," said Farber. "Just forget about Doc."

Carney saw Betsy Gaye on the edge of the crowd, wrapped in a cloak. He worked his way toward her as Farber began to give orders. He stood a pace away, waiting.

She said, "Who could lead a raid like this?"

"He's a medicine man. He uses fire a lot. His particular bunch think he's a god of some kind."

Her face was elongated with sadness in the flickering

light. "While I was singing and playing—they were dying. What kind of a world is it, Will?"

"Sometimes I wonder myself." His tone was flat. "They think highly of me in Sautelle tonight. I wonder how they'll feel tomorrow or the next day?"

There was a small wailing sound from the dirt street. Carney stared, then began to run. The bundle thrown away by the Apache he had shot last was stirring. Small arms protruded, waving. Carney snatched up the Shriver baby and stared at it, disbelieving.

Betsy reached and took it from him. "A baby!"

"They always steal children and make slaves of them," he said in awe. "Even on the run they tried to take the baby with them."

She turned and walked toward Main Street, looking tenderly down at the weeping child. "It'll be some consolation for the father."

Carney followed her. There was a sour taste in his mouth, he felt drained, despondent. Wherever he went there was shooting, there was trouble, there was death. He could not avoid it. There was no refuge for him.

Chapter Eight

IT WAS TWO o'clock in the morning, but they still sat around a table in Mrs. Margate's restaurant drinking coffee by the light of a single lamp, Carney and Farber and Betsy Gaye and Fuller, who had come struggling from needed sleep during the gunfire. They all looked up as the Reverend Peterson came in and walked slowly to where they waited.

"The miracle of the child," he said. "Marshal Shriver would not have survived, I think, had it not been for the recovery of his little son."

Farber said, "He'll be all right."

"Her brothers were here this afternoon. They will return tomorrow," said the preacher. "I will arrange for services."

"You do that," said Farber.

The aged man inclined his head, looking at each of them briefly, as though estimating their characters, then turned and departed.

"He spooks me," said Farber.

Mrs. Margate came with a fresh pot of steaming brew. "He's a good man. I've seen preachers who were not." For the moment there was an armed truce between her and Farber.

Fuller put sugar in his fresh cup of coffee and said, "It ain't like Apaches to raid a town like this. That Fireboy is loco, and so is the bucks with him. Did anybody send a message to the fort?"

"Yes," Carney told him. "I did. Shriver wasn't in any condition, so I took it on myself."

"There's a guard out," Farber said. "Not that town people can stop Apaches from getting where they want."

"Medicine men are all loco," Fuller went on. "This one is worse than most in some ways. He don't make any sense whatsoever. What could he get by burnin' this town? Sojers on his trail, that's what he could get. It don't make no sense, nohow."

Betsy Gaye spoke for the first time. "Death is always horrible to me. I've never been able to believe in the Hereafter, milk and honey and angels playing harps. Those poor people."

Carney stirred. "The Apaches are just as dead. Sure, they started it and they deserved it, but they're just as cold and stiff."

Madge Margate looked at him but said nothing. Fuller noisily sucked at his coffee.

"I think you should retire," Farber said formally to Betsy Gaye. "It's been too much. I'm terribly sorry it had to happen the night of your opening show. But the people liked you."

Betsy said, "Yes, I should go to bed." She arose, and Farber took her arm, more possessively now, as though he felt he was on surer ground. Carney watched them leave, his legs extended beneath the table, slouched in his

79

chair. She was careful not to glance his way. Farber strutted, and Mrs. Margate suddenly choked, coughing.

Fuller said, "I got to take that coach out at five. Thank ye for the brew, Miz Margate." He followed the other two across the street and into the hotel.

The woman put her elbows on the table and said, "Not sleepy, are you Carney?"

"No." He tapped his fingers on the checkered cloth. "How did your husband smell out the Apaches?"

"He can get around the hotel. His arms are very strong. He thinks it is apelike, the way he moves. He doesn't like to have anyone see him. He was at the rear window, the one where you saw me."

Carney raised his eyebrows.

"You mean why didn't he use the rifle?" She laughed in a short dry manner. "That's not Charlie's strongpoint. He called Milton and went to his room and crawled under the covers."

"Then he did see the Apaches before the fire started?"

"He uses binoculars. He sees more than anyone knows."

The implication was plain and inexcusable. One shot would have given the Apaches pause and aroused some part of the town much quicker. Carney thought about this. The woman sat silent for several minutes.

Carney said, "It must be tough on you."

"I'm almost used to it." She leaned back. "It gets to be a way of life. Nobody's perfect, it's just that some are less perfect than others."

"Most of us."

She said, "Amen."

He knew it was not an invitation. He had felt the force of her right from the start, but now he thought she was not challenging him, that she was debating something within herself.

"You and the girl," she said. "Betsy Gaye."

"I knew her some. In Tombstone."

"You knew Macie Grant?" Her voice was brittle, careful.

"Even less than Miss Gaye."

"You know about Macie Grant and Farber?"

80

Now it was his turn to be careful. "A little. Not much. She was killed in a buggy accident, wasn't she?"

"How much do you know about it—about them?"

"Nothing that wasn't in the Tombstone paper." That was true, he could look her in the eye. The rest was speculation on Betsy's part.

"You're not interested, are you?"

He waited a second, then said, "Maybe."

"You're a cautious man, Carney. Quick with a gun, but hard to get along with. And you're working for Cork Farber."

"You don't get along with Cork, I take it."

She laughed gently. "It's after two o'clock in the morning, and I think I killed an Indian tonight. My husband proved for the hundredth time that he's a coward. Cork is aiming straight at Miss Betsy Gaye and he always gets his woman. I've learned to trust only myself and then only part of the time. But I'm going to talk to you."

"I'm listening." Then he added, "Your husband did send for you. He did rouse the town."

"Too late to save Mrs. Shriver and her daughter. Don't tell me about Charlie, for God's sake, Carney, you don't have any idea . . ." She stopped.

"Okay." He waited. If she was going to talk, he had to listen. They were, in a way, in the same boat, she had an insoluble problem and she had to live with it, as he had to live with the ways of violence which were always in his path.

She said, "Macie Grant. A pretty little girl who was scared of just about everything. She was easy for Cork. She thought the sun rose and set in his hat. He took her up in his rooms to show her his collection of Indian jewelry." Her eyes flashed, she seemed to grow in size, sitting straight, talking past Carney, accusing. "He showed her, all right. What he didn't realize was that a scared girl who's been raped is dangerous. That she'd come to a woman with her story. He still doesn't know."

"Macie came to you?"

"The day she died. She told me about it, she knew that he didn't love her, that he only wanted to use her. That she was going to kill him."

81

"Did you warn Farber?"

"Me?" Now her laughter was wild. "Warn him? I loaned her a derringer!"

"Oh, I see." He did see, very plainly, in that moment.

"That's right, he threw me over for Macie Grant. That's the way he is. That's his weakness. Do you want to hear the rest?"

"I want to hear it."

She became calm, looking at him now, lowering her voice, speaking with deep feeling. "If you have anything for that girl, Betsy Gaye, get her out of here as soon as you can. Don't smile, Farber is that dangerous and that quick—with women."

Carney said, "To some kind of women."

She winced. "Believe me, Carney, I'm not that easy. Oh, I'm not one of your churchly, mealy-mouthed pioneer women. But I'm choosey and I'm usually careful. Not many people in Sautelle guessed about me and Farber—and only Doc Reynolds, that devil, really knew."

"I was going to ask about Doc. He strikes me as stronger than Farber, wasn't for the booze."

"If it wasn't for Doc, there might have been some hope for Cork," she said. Then she shook her head. "No, I shouldn't say that. They're a good pair. Farber takes the women, Doc cuts them up afterward with his sneers and insults."

"You were saying that Macie Grant came to you and borrowed a derringer."

"That was the day he took her for the drive."

"She wasn't alone in the buggy that day?"

"She was alone when the horse ran away. He was picking wildflowers for her. That's what he said. Picking wildflowers. But nobody ever mentioned the derringer."

Carney said, "Now, wait. You say she was ready to kill him. But they drove out, and she sat in the buggy while he went to pick flowers for her?"

"That's what Farber said and that's the way it stands."

"But she was scared of horses. She wouldn't sit in the buggy alone while he went into a field." He realized

82

he had revealed Betsy's confidence—but Madge didn't react.

She arched her shapely brows at him and said, "You see?" There was a smile on her face that was not pleasant. "Her head was so badly smashed that the coffin was closed at the funeral. If you care to go out there, where it happened, you'll find there is only one spot along that trail where rocks that big and that jagged can be found. Odd, isn't it?"

"It looks bad all right."

"They held an inquest. Death by accident, they said. Marshal Shriver picked the jury. Some friends and from the county he brought in his wife's brothers, the three Eggerlys."

Carney started. "Eggerly? Did you say Eggerly?"

"That was poor Mrs. Shriver's maiden name."

"And Cork knows this?"

"Certainly he knows it. Everyone knows it. The Eggerly name is very important in Arizona."

"Yeah," said Carney. "Yeah, it sure is." He thought of the girl, Macie, and he thought of Cork genially offering him aid because the Eggerlys were out to kill him, and he thought of Doc Reynolds and his drinking and his mocking way of quoting poetry. Then he thought about Betsy Gaye, who had come up here thinking to get some satisfaction about her girl friend and of what would happen to her at the hands of Farber and Reynolds if something weren't done about it.

The woman said, "It seems that you're involved with a lot of people, Carney."

"One way or another," he said, not really answering, just filling the gap in the conversation as his mind rotated, the irony biting deep into him, his flight here for escape and his belief he might have found a place to settle down, the immediate raid by Nok-e-da-klinne, now this revelation. It wasn't to be, he thought, there wasn't a chance for him to avoid violence and death and destruction.

She was going on, "That's the tragedy of life, to get involved with the wrong people. Like Charlie. Like Cork. And, if I would admit it, with me."

83

He looked at her, and her face seemed incredibly aged. All the laugh lines had turned in, gouged deeper. There were dark patches beneath her fine eyes. He forced his thoughts away from his own predicament.

"You've got a nice place here, Mrs. Margate. Your husband runs a good, clean hotel. Things could be a lot worse."

"Could they?" She seemed to be debating the point.

"From where I sit, they could be."

"It's all according to your point of view." She was quiet now, smiling a little. "You could say that I made my bed and should lie in it. You'd probably be right. But to me this is a living death. You needn't tell me that it is all my own doing. I know that. I still don't have to like it."

Her tone was quietly desperate. He was silent, thinking of what had to be done. She finished her coffee and stood up, and he rose as she went to the lamp and extinguished it. In semidarkness they moved across the restaurant to the door.

He said, "I'll have to do something about Farber. And the girl."

"Yes," she said. "You will. You're that kind of man."

"There's no proof against Cork."

She said, "The derringer I gave Macie Grant had a cross scratched on the plate on the left side. It was a Greek cross, not just an X."

"He could have thrown it away, buried it."

"He could have."

They stood in the doorway. There were a few lights in the town, aftermath of the excitement. He wondered what Dan Shriver was thinking, with only the boy child left of his family. There were no signs of life in the Cowboy Saloon. Mrs. Margate locked the door of the restaurant and turned toward him as they prepared to cross Main Street.

He caught the shock on her face, the alarm in her eyes, and instinctively he dropped to one knee, drawing his revolver, swinging around. He heard the whistle and thud of an arrow, he saw a dim figure alongside the hotel, the 2nd Street side. He fired—but missed, he knew.

84

He started to sprint after the fleeing Indian, then stopped so suddenly that he nearly fell.

He spun around, realizing what had happened, leaping back to the woman. He raised the Colt's and fired two quick shots in the air, then another. She was lying against the door of the restaurant, half upright, the arrow in her breast.

People came running, believing that the Apaches were back in force. Among them was Doc Reynolds, who carried a rifle.

Carney yelled, "Doc, here! Hurry!"

Mrs. Margate said, "Doc Reynolds. What an irony." Then she fainted.

A woman came in a dusty wrapper, and Carney ran toward 2nd Street, knowing it was too late, that the Apache had long since gone. He was well aware of the significance of the attack. The arrow had been for silence, the message had been, not for Mrs. Margate, but for him. Nok-e-da-klinne had marked him as the man who had prevented the destruction of Sautelle. Somehow in the hurly-burly he had been recognized.

Now he was marked for extinction by one more force in Arizona. The Apache medicine man would be on his trail, along with the Eggerlys.

He went back to where the crowd gathered around the woman. They were putting her on a shutter to carry her to the hotel. He saw Betsy Gaye's face at the window on the second floor. He followed the stretcher-bearers into the lobby.

Someone put a hand on his arm, and he looked into the drawn features of Dan Shriver. He allowed himself to be drawn aside.

The marshal said in a strained, low voice. "You saved the baby."

"Just happened that way." This was the brother-in-law of the Eggerlys, he must be very careful, he knew.

"It's all I got now. Y'all couldn't know what it means. I couldn't myself 'til it happened. Me and Ma, we got along real good. Yeah, real good."

"I'm sorry, Marshal."

"You saved the boy." He drew a deep whistling

85

breath. "I got to tell you, there'll be Eggerlys in town and three cousins. They'll come for the funeral. They got a few boys ridin' for 'em. It's a powerful bunch. You ain't got a chance agin 'em, Carney."

"I see." He could not let the man know that he had been warned by Mrs. Margate, he had to appreciate what Shriver was doing for him. "I sure am obliged."

"Cork Farber runs this town, you're onto that by now. Him and Doc, they don't cotton to the Eggerlys much, it's town agin country, like. But they can't save you. Simon's put out the word."

"I understand." He understood all too well. He had possibly a day to make Betsy Gaye safe, to take care of Farber and to make good at his flight. When he left Sautelle, there was every chance that Fireboy and his band would take up the trail.

It was then he thought of Mantocloz, across the border in Mexico. He remembered the place, the warm sun on faded adobe, the peace, the lush surroundings, the friendly faces of friends. He could go northward, true, to the Dakotas, to Montana, to Canada, but he was a man of the warm country, of the desert and the long days full of sunshine. If he could get back down to Tombstone, he might get across the river.

He might, if the Curly Bill Brocius bunch didn't get wind of his journey and lay for him. The situation was so complex and so impossible that he found himself grinning. It was a lopsided grin he carried into the hotel, as Shriver faded into shadows with the arrival of Cork Farber on the scene.

Shriver's last whispered words were, "Get outa town, Carney. I can't do nothin' more for y'all."

No one could do anything for him, Carney thought, walking across the small lobby through the people who gathered silently. Farber was at the desk, where Charlie Margate sat hunched in his chair. Carney stood behind him.

Margate said, "Doc says she might live. They won't let me in there." He gestured toward the room off the lobby with one long arm. "They are doing all they can. Is Doc sober?"

"He's sober and he'll pull her through if anyone can." This was the public Farber, the man of the future. with soothing, ingratiating manners for all, Carney realized. "The town owes you a vote of thanks, Charlie, you and Madge. We might all have been slaughtered if it wasn't for you."

A murmur of voices joined in assent. Farber gave them his boyish smile. Carney went up the stairs with his key. He needed to be alone and to think.

He was putting the key in the lock when Betsy Gaye came to his side in a flowing robe, her hair caught in a knot at the back of her head, her eyes wide and frightened. He opened the door, and they went into his room.

She asked, "Should I be helping? I'm a stranger and I saw the others gathered around—and I had to talk to you."

"You did right," said Carney. He knew his voice was heavy and toneless. Too much had happened too quickly.

"There's more to it than Mrs. Margate being hit by an arrow," Betsy Gaye said. "What is it, Will?"

He sat down heavily on the edge of the bed. He said, "What is it? I'll tell you what it is. There's all hell to pay with you and me in the middle."

"Macie?"

"She's in it—was in it. You better sit down. This is going to take a little while."

She perched opposite him on the bed. She was only a shape in the darkness now. He unbuckled his gunbelt, but as he told her the entire story he held it in his hands, as though reluctant to part with it even for a moment.

When he had finished, she said, "What are we going to do about it?"

"You better start packing. You can leave with Fuller in just a couple hours from now. Keep going, down country, back to Tombstone, maybe all the way back where you came from. Get yourself out of it and stay out of it."

"That's the wise thing to do, isn't it?"

"That's the only thing to do, believe me."

"And you? What will you do?"

87

"There's little time. It's not my job to do anything about Farber. I'll inform the Federal Marshal if I can. The only teeny little proof would be the derringer. And if Mrs. Margate dies, that's no good."

After a moment she said, "But you do believe he killed Macie, don't you?"

"I don't know. A jealous woman'll do anything to get even."

"That's true. But what do you really believe?"

"Maybe he killed her. I know he was set to use me against the Eggerlys or to put me in a bind where they'd get to me unless I did what he wanted. That's plain and simple. I can't gun him down for that."

"You never gunned anybody down, Will," she protested. "Not that way. Men came at you, and you protected yourself. I know that."

"You know it, and I know it. Nobody else would believe one little side of it. I'm headin' south. I'm getting out. I can't keep shooting people just to stay alive."

She said under her breath, "It's rotten. Both of us, running away."

"It's the way things are."

She shook her head. "It shouldn't be like that."

"Life's not tied up in neat bundles. It comes every which of a way."

"Yes. We've got to do something about it."

"Not 'we,'" he told her in alarm. "You'll be all right if you get away from Cork Farber."

"Will I?"

He stirred restlessly. "Nobody's going to shoot you. Just keep traveling. If you need money, I've got some."

"I don't want your money. You'll need every two-bit piece."

"Well, just go, then. Start packing, and I'll find Fuller and arrange for the trip."

"You do that," she said. She slid off the bed, and the springs creaked. She hesitated a moment, then repeated, "You do that. I'll meet you back here in an hour."

He got up and fastened the belt around his middle. She had opened the door and was listening. There were sounds below, the murmur of voices, the opening and closing of other doors.

She said, "In an hour, Will," and was gone.

He was glad that he had managed to sleep that afternoon. It was after three o'clock, and there was a good chance he would not see a bed that night. He went out of the room, locked it, and made his way down the back stairs and out of the hotel.

Again the town was quiet, the stars shining down at their brightest, giving some light to his way. Fuller was sleeping at the stage station beyond 4th Street, which was a couple of hundred yards from the Cowboy Saloon and on the same side of Main. Carney walked slowly, thinking about Betsy Gaye. The girl had courage, all right. She seemed also to have good basic common sense. He doubted that she had any funds and debated how much he should leave with the stage driver to see her through. He would have little use for money the way he was going, down through the back country, off the beaten paths toward Tombstone, between three and four hundred miles, he figured, of mountain and desert. He would need some funds to buy provisions when he dared and to keep a supply of ammunition, but that would not take nearly as much as he had in his oilskin packet.

Five hundred, he thought, would give her a good start. It would take her all the way back to Texas and leave her something over. She must have childhood friends back yonder. There must be some man who would marry her and give her a home. A girl like that ought not to be running loose around the frontier.

A sigh shook him from head to foot. He paused before the office of the stage company, behind which Fuller should be getting his slight sleep. If things had been different and he had met Betsy Gaye under proper circumstances and he was not on the run and . . . it was bootless even to think of it. His destiny was to move on and keep moving. He had never known any other way since he was a button. There was no reason to be looking

89

back now and certainly no opportunity of looking forward to other than repetition of the same old way of life.

He shook himself like a pup coming out of water and went in to awaken Fuller.

Chapter Nine

IN THE ROOM where the Margates lived Dr. Robert Reynolds rinsed his bloody hands over a white basin of carmined water. Milton held the bowl, his hands steady, his eyes remaining upon the woman who lay stretched before them. She was conscious, her face twisted with pain. The broken arrow lay upon a low bureau against the wall. Charlie sat in a basket chair, his powerful shoulders slumped. Two lamps burned brightly. The bandage was very white upon the woman's firm, tawny skin.

She said, "I'll live."

"Yes," said Dr. Reynolds. His receding chin was sunk into his neck, his mouth was bounded with elliptical lines. "You'll be laid up for a while, though. It tipped your lung."

"I know, I saw the blood. It was too bright . . . too bright." She weakly turned her head to her husband. "Were you worried, Charlie?"

"Not when I saw Dr. Reynolds work," said Charlie.

Madge went on, to the others. "Charlie studied medicine. You didn't know that, did you?"

Reynolds raised his eyebrows. "I didn't know. But his training will come in handy. He can tell Milton what to do."

"No," said Charlie. He heaved himself up from the chair, grasping two sticks that he had cunningly contrived, carven wooden handles supporting his forearms and wrists. "No, I'll attend to her. Milton will watch the restaurant."

Reynolds said, "She'll need constant care."

"Yes, Doctor," Charlie said formally. "I am deeply grateful for your services. Your skill is formidable."

"Thank you." Reynolds began replacing instruments in his bag. From the moment he had begun to work over the woman, he had altered his usual demeanor, had become coldly impersonal, swiftly efficient. Now he glanced around, sniffing a bit in disdain at the Spartan simplicity of the furnishings, then fastened his gaze upon Charlie. "You have a nerve injury, I take it?"

"Deterioration of muscle tissue, I'm afraid. Result of an injury. But I can get around." He hobbled a few steps. "Do you think I might improve with exercise?"

"If you are willing to endure some pain," said Reynolds. He nodded toward the bed. "She'll need full attention for a few days, you understand. You'd better get a woman to help."

"I'll do that." Charlie took out a fat leather pouch. "How much do I owe you, Doctor?"

Reynolds shrugged into his coat and picked up the bag. "How much is your wife worth to you?"

Charlie said in an even voice, "More than I would have believed." He dropped the pouch on the dresser top. "Help yourself, there's plenty in there."

Reynolds threw back his head, looking out from under heavy lids at the woman, then at Milton, then at the crippled big man. He weighed the moneybag in his hand. His voice changed, acquiring the rasp well known to them all. " 'Who steals my purse steals trash, something, something . . . But he that filches from me my good name, robs me of that which not enriches him, and makes me poor indeed.' Later it is said, 'It is the green-eyed monster which doth mock the meat it feeds on: that cuckold lives in bliss who certain of his fate loves not his wronger . . .' And so forth and so on." He dropped the purse and made the motion of washing his hand. "I'll stop by tomorrow. Good night, all."

Charlie Margate's voice blasted at him, "No, thank you, Doctor Reynolds. Take your fee. We won't be needing you further."

"Ha? It is so?" The sneer broadened. He picked up the moneybag and stuck it in his pocket. "In that case, let me assume that the laborer is worthy of his hire. If she hemorrhages, Doctor Margate, what then?"

The woman on the bed said strongly, "Why, I'll die, Doctor Reynolds. But it won't happen. Not yet. Good night, and I add my thanks for your services."

Reynolds seemed about to say more, but Milton opened the bedroom door, and the three, unified, stared him down. Muttering, he swaggered out.

Charlie said, "See him to the street, Milton. And make sure everything is secure. Then you can go to bed."

Milton batted his wide-spaced eyes and vanished. Charlie Margate, balancing himself with great care, crossed to the bed, leaned on his canes, and looked down at his wife.

She said, "You gave him all the money."

"Every last farthing."

"All you had saved for your escape."

"I had no further use for it."

She swallowed hard, and he hobbled to a carafe and brought water. She drank, sipping, reflecting.

"That was quite a line you read the good doctor," She said, raising her brows, smiling a little, unsure.

"I found that I meant it. When they brought you in, with that arrow in your breast . . . it was like a blow on the head. Scenes unwound in my mind. I can't explain it, Madge." He rubbed one hand over his bald head. "I can't understand it. But there it was."

"It was there." She shook her head slowly in amazement.

"I've been living inside me, for me, for nothing else all these years. Suddenly I realized how it has been for you. I . . . I don't believe in revelation . . . in miracles, however minor . . . or do I?"

"You reduced Doctor Reynolds. He was hacked, oh, how he was hacked! He wished he hadn't picked up the money."

"The money is a symbol . . . as he quoted, it's trash."

She managed a small laugh. "Charlie."

"Yes—dear?"

"About the money."

"It doesn't matter." His voice was low. "If you can forgive me, Madge."

"Forgive you? I've got a cache of my own. The restaurant has been far more profitable than you know."

After a moment he chuckled. "Of course. You're a very clever woman, Madge."

She reached out a shaky hand. "We can make it, right here in Sautelle. Doc and Cork Farber can't stop us from making it. There'll be new people, all will be forgotten in a few years."

He said, "We can make it if we want to." He held her hand a moment, then went back to his chair. "You've got to rest, sleep a lot. I'll be watching."

She closed her eyes. "Yes. I can sleep now. We can make it, Charlie . . . We . . . can . . . make it."

He sat and listened to her slow, labored breathing. If she lived, he thought, they would try. He knew very well that there was no certainty about her recovery, but this high country would be good for her, especially if the lung was affected. He was bemused with himself, putting her first, not concerned with Charlie Margate. He hoped he could live that way. It would be a good life for him, minus his fears, his unrest, his hatred.

He heard Milton go out onto the street. The hotel was almost empty, there was no danger of further excitement that night, he hoped. He settled deep into the chair, watching his wife's face by the lamplight. He wondered only briefly what Milton was doing out at this hour of the morning.

As Milton ran in his hobbledehoy fashion down Main Street from the hotel toward the Cowboy Saloon this was one of the few things he knew and could retain—why he was out at that hour of the morning. He made as little noise as possible. He wiped at his streaming eyes—he was not weeping, he was merely excited.

He had not fully grasped everything that went on in the sickroom at the hotel, but the gist of it was clear enough to him. His heroine, his secret mother, Madge Margate, had somehow managed to put down Doc Rey-

93

nolds, with the aid of Charlie. Milton had never expected to see this happen.

Now he wanted to find Carney, for whom he felt some mysterious affinity. Perhaps he had heard men in bars talking about the gunfighter, about his beginnings as a ward of whoever would have him for the moment. Milton also had no family. The difference lay in the fact that he knew that when he had wandered from the wagon train, nobody cared. They had not bothered to search for him, those slatternly people among whose brood he belonged. Or never had belonged, because his wits had been slow and his speech impeded, he thought. He had been quite small and knew only his given name, or by some quirk refused to recall the name of the family that had rejected him.

How he had survived was something no one could know. He had eaten insects, the bark of trees, roots of weeds. He had worked on farms, in kitchens, somehow making his way to Sautelle. Here he had found Madge Margate, and she had taken him in. He thought her the most beautiful woman in the world.

She had cleaned him up, taught him how to do things, made him useful. Charlie had complained a lot at first, but finally Milton was able to help the crippled man, too. He felt himself a real citizen until the business of Mrs. Margate and Cork Farber had come to his attention.

Being uneducated and uncomprehending of social usage, he was not affected by the moral aspect of the affair between his idol and the saloonkeeper. However, when he knew that Farber had discarded Madge and in so doing had diminished her, the wish to kill had established itself in him. Cork Farber became a man Milton wanted to remove from earth.

Doc Reynolds, with his jeering and cruelty became a secondary target only because Mrs. Margate seemed to suffer from his jibes. Milton could not possibly know exactly how Doc managed it, he only knew that she was often hurt and that Doc was responsible.

Now, as he loped along looking for Carney, he knew that the new lady, Miss Betsy, was not in her room, that Carney was somewhere around in the quiet darkness, and that Reynolds and Farber were dangerous to all concerned. He had to get to Carney to tell him something. He was not quite certain why he had to do this or precisely what he had to tell, but he knew it was important. To Milton there were only two sides to a question, and always Madge Margate was on the right side, just as Cork Farber was on the wrong side. Further, he sensed that the new lady and Carney were now against the enemy. Milton's cerebration was weak, but his instincts were powerful.

He was also adept at a certain protective coloration in that he could be upon a scene without being noticed. He had developed this over years of preferring to remain invisible lest he be put upon by quicker wits. Thus his powers of observation were acute. When he saw the strong light, wick turned up full, in the Cowboy Saloon, he knew someone therein was awake. He crossed the street, stooping low, and ran lightly onto the verandah, cautiously peering through a window.

The shade was nearly drawn, but he applied his eyes to a crack and could see deep into the big barroom to the rear, where the tables surrounded the dais upon which Miss Betsy Gaye's performance had been given.

He saw her sitting at one of these tables. Her position was unnaturally rigid. Opposite her Cork Farber lounged as though he were in a poker game. Milton had seen him like this before, pretending to be half asleep, actually as alert as a hunted fox.

Then Milton's eyes grew wide and round. Miss Betsy was holding a derringer in her right hand. It was pointed at Farber. And in the far background, concealed from the pair at the table, Doc Reynolds leaned against a wall.

Milton ran back down the steps to the street, looking wildly up and down. Miss Betsy held the gun, but Doc Reynolds held the key, he knew. He raised his hands to heaven, imploring help. None was in sight.

He scuttled up the alley between the saloon and the Wells Fargo office. This was a place he remembered from previous spying excursions upon Farber and Doc. He found the window that opened into the ladies parlor. It was imperfect and could not be secured. He began working at it, his hands shaking, fear in his bowels, striving to make no sound.

The window inched up. Milton reached inside and found the stick used to prop it into place. He was sweating and had trouble controlling his breathing. He pulled himself up headfirst, fell over the sill. He managed to squirm into the ladies parlor. He sat for a moment, removing his boots to make sure he would not make any noise. He crawled toward the saloon.

He was stopped dead by the beaded portieres. If he as much as breathed upon them, they would give off a familiar tinkling sound. He gathered his legs beneath him and crouched like an animal at bay. He could hear them talking and he could dimly see Doc Reynolds against the wall.

Betsy Gaye was saying, "You killed her."

"No, I did not kill her," Cork Farber answered.

"I'm going to take you to the marshal," Betsy said. Her voice was strong enough, but Milton thought she had to be at least skittery.

"And I told you I will not go," said Cork. "What do you propose to do? Shoot me in cold blood?"

She said, "Someone will come here. Carney is awake. You killed her and you'll pay."

"Will Carney is my friend. He won't believe I killed Macie Grant. He knows me better than that."

She said, "You'll stand trial, Farber. I swear it."

"I did not kill her." Milton could see Reynolds in the background. Reynolds was stalling, afraid to move for fear Betsy Gaye would fire the little gun, he realized. It was a cat and mouse game, and behind the portieres he wondered how he could take part in it. His knees hurt, and he thought he was getting a cramp in his right foot.

Farber said, "Try and see it my way, please. Macie gave me that derringer. We were very fond of each other. It was a terrible shock to me when she was killed."

"I don't believe you."

"You can't just sit there. Your hand is getting tired right now. Remember, this is my town. Even if someone came along, you wouldn't be believed. In fact, I could have you arrested for sneaking into my room and stealing that gun."

She said, "I'll take that chance."

Farber shook his head. "It's a long wait until morning. I can stand it if you can."

He wouldn't be so brave, Milton thought, if he did not know that Doc Reynolds was there, waiting to take his part. It was true that the new lady couldn't hold that little gun steady very much longer. If only Milton had a weapon—but, then, he had never shot off a gun of any kind. And how could he take a chance on hitting Miss Betsy? No, he could only wait and see what happened. He glued his eyes upon Doc, listening to the conversation at the table, not quite comprehending its full import but knowing that the girl was in dire trouble. How he hated the two smug men, always on the winning side, able to harm Mrs. Margate or anyone else in Sautelle. He rubbed his stockinged foot to start the blood to circulating. There were beads of sweat on his forehead, on his lip.

Betsy Gaye was nervous. "You'd better get up and walk out of here, Farber."

"I'm not about to," he told her.

"If my hand does get tired, my finger might slip," she said.

"That's your problem." He was fully at ease, smiling at her. "It would be murder, you know."

"As your friend the doctor would say, 'An eye for an eye, a tooth for a tooth.'"

At the mention of his name Doc Reynolds leaned away from the wall. As Milton watched with horrified eyes Reynolds took a razor from his breast pocket and began moving forward with soft, noiseless steps. The light fell across his face, the purpose plain in the set of his inconsiderable chin, the straight line of his thin lips. Milton poised like a sprinter but was held in the sliver of time by knowledge that Farber would move in tune with his partner, that the girl could be, would likely be, killed in the confusion.

Then, catching a glimpse of Doc's eyes, he knew that in any case she would be killed. There was no mistaking the intent of that shining, poised blade, aimed at

97

her exposed white neck. Even Farber changed expression, was alarmed, regretful, frightened, yet knowing of the alternatives.

Reynolds moved nearer and nearer. Betsy held the derringer aimed straight at Farber. There was a tiny amount of time left, no more. Milton heaved a sobbing breath and charged forward, all arms and legs, shouting, "Shoot him, Miss, shoot him!"

Reynolds wheeled, and the boy ran smack into him, arms windmilling with no direction but with considerable force. Reynolds was borne backward, not knowing his assailant, not realizing the ease with which he might turn the tide, striving for balance, losing it, crashing down so that his head hit the corner of the platform with a sickening thud.

Cork Farber had hooked the leg of the table with his toe. Now he jerked it toward him, at the same time ducking away. Betsy, her elbow propped, was sent forward, so that her upper body lay on the careening table top. Farber slithered back to grab the derringer from her hand.

When she recovered herself, Farber was covering her with the gun, calling, "Nice work, Doc."

There was no reply save the labored breathing of Milton. Farber edged around so that he could keep Betsy in his eye and manage to survey the scene.

"Doc!"

Milton huddled on the floor, spent. He had used up all his strength, he was useless now, a sodden heap. The razor lay a foot from his hand, but he made no attempt to pick it up.

Farber said, "Milton, you damn fool. By God, you'll do as I say, now. Get hold of Doc, drag him over here."

But Milton could not move. He was paralyzed, his vague face turned toward Betsy, full of guilt because he had failed her, woeful in the knowledge of impending death. He had managed his small moment, now his world was collapsed.

Farber said, "By God, I'll kill you both if you don't do as I say."

Betsy was standing straight, away from the table.

98

Her cheeks were very white, but her eyes flashed fire. "Kill, Farber, kill. That's all you know."

"I didn't kill your damned girl friend," he said. A bit of froth appeared at the corner of his mouth. "Everything was going all right until you came busting in here." He called plaintively, "Doc, wake up. We've got to get rid of these two."

Doc lay in a heap, unmoving. Milton could not stir. Farber looked right and left, at the door, at the ladies' parlor, where the portiere lay torn under Milton's charge. This was his palace, his home, everything of his future. It could vanish within the next hour if he did not behave correctly, if his instinct for self-preservation went wrong. He drew his own gun, putting the little derringer in his pocket, seeking solace in the bigger weapon and its walnut butt.

"Get over there, you," he said to Betsy. "Get with your friend, beside him."

She moved slowly, knowing he was above and beyond his tolerance, that he would shoot them both if he thought it was necessary. She bent and lifted Milton to his feet, feeling the tremors of his thin body, smelling the fear in him.

Keeping them at bay, Farber bent to the razor. It came naturally to his left hand. He had seen Doc use it as an emergency scalpel more than once. He remembered that blood seldom spurted, that the flesh parted as though by magic beneath the caress of the blade. He went forward on the balls of his feet, a flush on his cheeks, following the girl as she supported Milton.

From the ladies' parlor Carney said, "Drop it, Cork."

He swung around, the razor in one hand, revolver in the other. He fired offhand. Then he was struck in the chest, a blow that sent him spinning and falling and cursing into a deep gully, softly floating, then landing with a force that sent the strength from him, so that both blade and gun fell from flaccid grasp, and he lay staring up at the man who stood over him, looking somberly down, sadly brooding.

From afar off, Cork said, "I didn't kill the girl. It was . . . it was . . ." He could not finish.

99

Betsy Gaye cried, "The derringer. I found it in his room. It's in his pocket."

Carney bent and removed the small gun, turning it in the light. The Greek cross was plain to see. He rose and said, "Better get out of here. We can talk later."

She pointed to Reynolds. "He came at me with the razor, then Farber . . . but it was Milton who saved me."

"Outside," said Carney. He did not like it in the saloon. He saw that Reynolds was unconscious, bleeding from the skull injury. The shots would awaken someone, he was certain. He led them back to the window, shoved the shivering boy through, then aided Betsy to manage her skirts.

He looked back at the place in which he had hoped to work for a while, to gain time, to establish a new existence. The two men lay on the floor without stirring, one dead, one badly hurt. Another chapter had ended here.

He threw a leg over the windowsill and ducked out and dropped to earth. Milton was recovering equilibrium, Betsy was trying to tell him what had happened. He silenced them and went to the mouth of the alley. There were lights where none had been before.

He said. "Back to the hotel. Hurry!"

He made them run down Main Street. If they were seen and recognized, there might be immediate trouble for them all. The derringer in his pocket was not enough, he knew. Reynolds was still alive to deny everything for himself and his dead partner. Farber's dying words had been a denial of guilt.

Charlie Margate met them in the lobby, anxious, propping himself on the cane-crutches. "I heard the shot. What happened to Milton?"

"He saved me," Betsy said. "They were going to kill me, and Milton saved me."

"Farber's dead." Carney looked curiously at Margate, noting the change in him, in his attitude, in his straightforward glance. "Can you protect Milton?"

"We have friends, I believe," said Charlie. "What about you?"

"There are Eggerlys coming in," said Carney. "I've got to run. Betsy will have to take the stage."

"I can't do that!"

"I've already paid your passage," Carney told her. "Fuller will take care of you. Go upstairs and pack. I'll see that the stage leaves early."

Charlie Margate said, "Could you talk to Madge before you leave?"

"Certainly." Carney scowled at Betsy. "You'd best go and get ready right now."

She looked at him for a long moment. Her lips moved, but no sound came from her. She reminded him of a small girl who had been told she could not attend the Sunday School picnic. Her eyes were full of sad speculation, then she dropped long lashes and nodded. She turned away and went up the stairs. He watched her slim ankles flashing beneath the long skirt, and within him something stirred, and he felt cold, as though a wind had blown into the hotel. He followed Charlie and Milton with wrenching regret gnawing at him.

The woman was pallid, lying in the bed, but her voice was strong. "Farber?" she asked.

"Farber. And Reynolds has a bleeding skull," said he. "It was sudden. They meant to kill Betsy. Milton can tell you about it."

Milton said, "C-C-Carney was just in t-time."

"Betsy found your derringer." He showed it to her. "Farber claimed he didn't kill Macie Grant."

Milton cried, "B-b-but he didn't!"

"He must have," Madge Margate said, but there was panic in her gaze. "Carney! He did kill her!"

Milton was red-faced, abashed, one foot already retreating, face averted, moving toward the door. "F-F-Farber took the little pistol from her. D-D-Doc hit her with the rock."

"You saw this?" demanded Carney.

"I-I-I was there." He squirmed in agony. "W-W-Watchin' Doc. H-H-He was sneakin' after 'em on that pony."

"They fought over the derringer," Carney said speculatively. "Farber pushed Macie Grant out of the buggy among the rocks. The horse took the bit and ran. Right?"

Milton nodded. "D-D-Doc hit her. Hard. Th-Th-Then he rode back to t-t-town."

"Farber didn't know that Doc killed the girl?"

"F-F-Farber pushed her outa the carriage," Milton said. "Wh-Wh-When he come back, she was dead."

Carney shrugged, suddenly utterly weary with violent death. He said to Madge, "Farber would have killed Betsy. It was in him to do it. She'd scared him with her threats. I don't think Doc will be much good to himself or anybody. His head's caved in pretty bad. This was a town I thought might be nice and quiet. I'll have to say adios, now."

"I'm sorry, Carney," said Madge. She closed her eyes. She looked older than her years. "I'm really sorry."

He left the three of them together, going across the lobby and up to his room. He packed with care. He shouldered his bedroll and carried the rifle and saddlebag, moving swiftly now, going down the back way, anxious to avoid seeing Betsy Gaye again, depending upon Fuller to take care of her.

There were people stirring in the streets, he heard Dan Shriver's voice as the marshal tried to keep order. There would be a posse as soon as it was known that Carney had disappeared, there would be Eggerlys to lead. Until then, he thought, it would be a mystery, unless Reynolds should regain consciousness. He had seen many head injuries and he would be surprised if the doctor survived.

He went into the stable and found it deserted as he saddled Star and arranged his bedroll. The voices down the street became louder. He tied up the black for a moment, unable to restrain his curiosity. Perhaps he regretted leaving town, taking it on the run so soon, at any rate. He walked in the shadows toward the sounds in the night.

He heard a loud voice demand, "What did Doc say? Who done it? Let's get started here."

Dan Shriver answered, "Doc didn't make much sense. He died before he could rightly say who done it."

Now, Carney thought, perhaps he should round up Betsy Gaye and reconsider the plans. Perhaps she could remain in Sautelle.

The first voice persisted, "Come on, now marshal, I heard him say somethin'. It musta been about the killer."

"Farber was a good man," chimed in another. "Somebody said that new gal was with him. What about her?"

Shriver said, "I know she was with him. I'm just before askin' her some questions."

"And where's Carney?" another voice demanded. "He was around an hour ago. How come Madge Margate got hurt when she was with him? How come the 'Paches come in on us after he gets in town?"

"Get the gal," the other demanded. "This town's had enough. Time we done somethin'."

That was the predominant thinking of the crowd, Carney knew. In a moment it could be a mob. He turned back to the stable. It was time to get out. He stood a moment at the head of Star, estimating time. There was no sign of activity at the Wells Fargo office. The stage station was empty. Fuller was not in sight. Where was Betsy Gaye? Shriver would be looking for her whether he wanted to or not. His highly developed sense of danger kept him motionless, all senses straining. He heard running footsteps and whisked the rifle out of its scabbard, leaping into shadows behind the horse.

Two figures ran into the yard. One was Milton, awkward as ever, carrying a bedroll. The other was smaller, wearing boots and heavy Levis turned up at the bottom and a short coat. There was no mistaking the way she moved—it was Betsy Gaye.

Carney said, "Have you gone out of your mind altogether?"

Milton wheezed and gasped, "Th-Th-They're in town. Th-Th-The Eggerly boys."

"What of it?" asked Carney. "It'll take them plenty of time to find out everything and get organized. Shriver is in no hurry to set them onto me."

Betsy said, "They're looking for me, too. Simon Eggerly sent them a message to look out for you and me, that I had something to do with you getting away in Tucson."

"He can't know that for sure."

103

"Does it make any difference to an Eggerly if he's sure or not? I'm going with you, Will."

"Oh, no, you're not doing anything of the kind!" But he knew she was right. She could not take the stage to Tucson if Simon Eggerly could in any way connect her with Will Carney. He stood a moment, helpless. Then he said weakly, "We haven't got a chance. You couldn't manage the ride. Even if we had a horse for you, which we ain't."

Milton said, "C-C-Carney, there's a good bay pony. D-D-Doc won't need it no more."

Betsy came close to him. "I was raised on a ranch. I can make any ride you can make. If you don't want me along, I'll go by myself. I'm scared of the Eggerlys, I can't help it. There's too many of them."

Milton was already struggling with a saddle. Carney went to his aid, moving as if in a nightmare now. The voices down the street were getting louder. He heard someone curse Dan Shriver and knew that the marshal was stalling because of the baby Carney had saved from the Apaches.

"A woman hasn't any notion to be lynched, either," Betsy said. She tightened the cinch herself. The bay horse was a good-looking animal with a stout barrel, not a fancy horse but one with bottom. She swung up the bedroll, and Carney affixed it for her.

She said, "Don't worry about me. Just show me the way, and I'll be right behind you. But hurry, please."

It was time to go, all right. He shook Milton's hand and said, "You've been a good friend, boy. Take care of Mrs. Margate."

"G-G-Good-bye, Carney," said Milton. "G-G-Good luck."

The girl made a standing mount without aid, and he could see by the way she managed the strange horse that she could make it—for a while, at least. Carney got aboard Star and reined him sharply, curbing all non-sense, heading him for the back lots, paralleling Main Street, eastward of town. It seemed impossible that he had not been in Sautelle thirty-six hours.

Fuller wheeled the stage up to the station and sat

104

a moment, staring at the crowd. Down between the Cowboy Saloon and the stable Carney could see him perched on the box, undecided what to do. It was then he thought of the five hundred dollars he had given the old driver. He laughed without humor. He would miss that money someday—if he lived.

Chapter Ten

THE EGGERLYS, Bo, Jack, and Peter, and their cousins Flint, Slater, and Patton sat in the lobby of the Margate House. Peter was the leader and spokesman. They were all heavy of jaw and narrow of eye, but there were differences among them, they were not knitted together by the absent Simon, they were geographically apart and were prospering in this section of Arizona. Dan Shriver told them all that had happened since the advent of Carney.

"He saved my baby," the marshal told them. "I got to tell y'all, that means somethin' to me."

Peter surveyed him with a mixture of contempt and pity. "You got a right."

"He hadda get Farber and Doc on account of the gal. I got to tell you all, the Margates and him just about saved the town. That means the bank where your money is and a whole hell of a lot of other things." Shriver was sweating. If they disagreed, he could be dead, before morning. He wondered if he cared. He had found the hiding place in the brick chimney and rescued the gold coins, but the paper money was charred beyond salvation. He had to hold on in Sautelle or take his child elsewhere and start anew and he was not likely to find such a place for his talents. "I got the people calmed down. They was all for lynchin'. You know that ain't good for a town."

105

The Eggerly clan communicated silently with each other, eyes rolling. Bo said, "Simon wants Carney."

Charlie Margate hunched from behind the desk on his canes. "That should be a matter for Simon and his immediate family. You know, Peter, that if you follow Carney, some of you will not return."

"Us Eggerlys got our pride," Peter said. "Carney killed some of us, he might kill more. That is as it may be. Simon's the head of the family. His word goes."

"That's right," agreed Jack. "That's the way it's got to be."

Dan Shriver looked at Peter. "You admit I don't have to go?"

"You got your rights," agreed Peter. "Sis put a lot of store in you." It was obvious he did not agree, but he was trying to be fair. "And you got your duty here. The town's in a stew, no question about it."

Charlie Margate interposed gently, "There's still the burial of your sister."

"There's that," said Peter.

"A good many people feel Carney done them a big favor," Shriver said.

"Farber and Reynolds were milking the miners. Nobody is going to miss them. I can handle any medical emergencies until we get a new doctor," Margate told them.

Peter Eggerly said, "Seems like Carney made a lot of friends in a hurry. This is somethin' we'll have to augur about, me and the boys."

He led them out of the hotel and down toward the Cowboy Saloon. Business was as usual in that place, with Chico the bartender officiating until disposition of the property could be made. D. Brand and Ed Leeds, the town leaders now, were already on the premises, estimating their position in view of the demise of the two men they had learned to respect and fear.

Milton came from the depths of the hotel. Charlie Margate led him silently into the room where Madge lay on her back, listening to all that took place.

She looked at her husband, smiling. "You did well,

106

Charlie. You spoke just enough and you said the right things. It was a good performance."

"Thank you, my dear." He put a hand on her brow. "Your fever has subsided."

She closed her eyes, the smile lingering. "Carney will get away. If they'd gone right out after him, it might have been different. The girl will slow him down. But given a start, he'll make it."

"Go where?"

"Never mind that," she said. "The girl will show him the way."

Milton said timidly, "C-C-Carney is a good man, ain't he, Miz Margate?"

"We think so." She opened her eyes, looking at her husband. "Don't we, Charlie?"

"Yes, we do," he said. "And you're a good boy, Milton. But don't ever tell anyone it was you who took care of Doc Reynolds."

Milton looked scared. "M-M-Me? Th-th-that was a accident, Mr. Margate. I-I-I druther be dead than tell anybody."

"You did what you had to do," Mrs. Margate said gently. "You're a fine boy. We want you to always stay with us. And you're going to run the restaurant while I'm laid up, just as I've taught you."

Milton straightened his lank frame. "I'm gonna try, honest I am. I'm gonna bust a gut tryin'!"

In the Cowboy Saloon, the Eggerly clan was conferring with the banker and the proprietor of the general store. Somehow, they realized, they were, in spite of the recent tragedies, speaking with lighter hearts and nimbler tongues than in previous meetings. If they did not mention this, they were still inwardly aware of it.

Ed Leeds ventured, "About Carney and the girl. You won't get anybody from town to go after them. I'm sorry, Peter, but we believe in let well enough alone. They done some good here and maybe they done some bad. We're for lettin' them find their own punishment or salvation as the case may be."

There was a silence. Feet shifted on the floor, spurs scraped. Chico the bartender stopped polishing the mahogany and looked off into space. Peter rubbed his long nose. When he spoke, it was with great solemnity, as though handing down a decision from on high.

"Well, now, we already talked with the Margates at the hotel. Seems like they agreed with you folks. Thing is, we want to live hereabouts and do business with Sautelle and raise up our families decent. On t'other hand, there is Simon, down South, and he's got a whiplash reaches a powerful distance."

Banker Brand blinked. "What Peter says is correct. There's Simon Eggerly money in the mines, in the ranches. We hold a lot of paper backed by him."

Ed Leeds began to look stubborn. He was a New England storekeeper, and his mulishness was well known in Sautelle. "I still say nobody's gonna ride with you."

Peter ignored him. "We got to bury our sister, natur'ly. That's first off."

The local men relaxed, smiling.

Peter went on, "Then we'll make a run. Just so's you understand. We'll most likely never pick up a trail by then. Carney moves fast."

The banker said smoothly, "And we can let it be known that you did your level best to get Carney, but he headed south, and it's up to Simon to head him off."

"You got a good head on your shoulders, Brand," Peter told him. "One hand washes the other, we'll all get along purty good hereabouts. Am I right?"

"You are right," he said, winking at Ed Leeds. "Now, about this property here. I suggest the bank take over and administrate it until the search for heirs is completed. Lacking heirs, the Territory will have jurisdiction, of course. What I'm thinkin', the money made should be held in trust, and out of it comes a fee. Now, to my way of thinkin', this fee could be applied to all those who lost property or life durin' the Apache fight. We got to think of the town as a group of people, like a family." He paused, grinned. "Like the Eggerlys?"

Peter said solemnly, "You got somethin' there, Brand. You couldn't do better."

They repaired to the bar for a libation. The bloodstains on the floor where Farber had fallen were almost

108

invisible, in case anyone noticed. Chico worked like a beaver, determined to hold onto his job, estimating how much he could steal from the damper.

Apart from the others, Bo Eggerly whispered to Peter, "It's kinda risky, at that. Not goin' out after Carney."

"You know better'n that," Peter told him.

"How can we be sure, though?"

"You heard Injun Jim."

"I heard him, but can we believe him?"

"He's a Navajo, he ain't no Apache. When he says Fireboy is out there layin' for Carney, you can believe him."

Bo Eggerly drank his whiskey slowly, looking off into space. Then he said, "You know what? This Carney, from what people say, he ain't such a bad hombre."

"Never met the man," said Peter, shrugging.

"Me, neither. But I'm right sorry for him. That 'Pache's got tricks with fire I hate to even think about."

"Like he's pullin' out our chestnuts?" Peter Eggerly laughed.

Chapter Eleven

FAR TO THE EAST and south of Sautelle the two horses labored into a stand of pine atop a plateau in the foothills of the White Mountains. There was a stream below, known as Arrio Creek, which ran into the Black River below Fort Apache. Cibicu, the Apache Reservation, was too close for comfort, but Carney had ideas on this subject, knowing the Apache mind from childhood, surmising that Nok-e-da-klinne might possibly return for reinforcements after the debacle at Sautelle, surmising that his hold over the tribesmen needed strengthening.

This was high ground for that vicinity, and he was satisfied to make camp. It was late afternoon, and the girl drooped, her shoulders narrowed, her chin down.

He had shown no mercy to her nor to the horses. The posse he expected from Sautelle had not appeared, but he had not relinquished an iota of wariness lest they should press on without rest toward the fort. Surely they must know that this was his only port of safety, the place where he must stock up for any journey he might choose.

He swung down and caught Betsy as she fell from the bay. Her legs buckled under her as he lowered her to the earth.

"Give me another day or so," she muttered. "Haven't been on a horse in too long."

He said, "The first day is the toughest. We'll make a cold camp, just in case."

"If I can lie down. Everything is going in circles."

He took a blanket from his bedroll and spread it beneath a tall tree. His mind was going through orderly channels that had been hewn by long practice. He noted with surface attention that there were circles beneath her eyes and that she was quite pale. He did not know what to do about it, there was only safety in hurried flight, there was no time to compromise.

He said uneasily, "Just lay there awhile. I got to climb the tree before dark."

He went to his saddlebag and rummaged for an old collapsible spyglass he had acquired somewhere along the line of his lifetime retreat. He removed his spurs and began climbing the accommodating pine with its ladderlike projecting limbs. He was not very good at scaling trees, but he puffed and hauled his way to a position where he could prop himself against the main trunk and adjust his glass.

He could see the road, which they had deserted long before the ride across country to this place. He could see every westerly point of the compass. There was only wildlife, moving through the grama grass, nibbling at the vegetation. This was country that would someday be cattle land, when the nearby Apaches were convinced that raids only led to extermination of their breed. A sawmill, he thought idly, to clear the pine and the oak and the aspen and juniper and manzanita and make use of the wood for building or for heating, that would be a good idea for a man willing to work.

He laughed at himself. There was no sawmill in his future, only hitting and running. Off to the southwest he thought he saw something moving in the forest of oak, but several moments later he could not be certain. He blinked his eyes, looked away, then back at this spot. He was well aware of Apache caution, how they would use every method of protective coloration even when they were sure that no enemy lurked. He wondered if by now their unbelievable underground communications had informed Nok-e-da-klinne that Carney had taken to the road again.

It would be a rough road this time. If he did not have the responsibility of the girl, it would be simple enough, perhaps. He could ride through to Fort Apache, rest awhile in comparative safety, then flee south, where the Eggerlys would least suspect him to go. Now he was thinking of Riley, in Mantocloz. The Mexican ranchero beckoned. Now he was convinced that no place in Arizona or anywhere north of the Border would be safe for him as long as an Eggerly was alive.

It had come as a shock, riding out of Sautelle, when this certainty struck him. It had made him moody and silent through the day. His conscience smote him because it had also distracted him from the girl and her plight. He began to descend from the pine tree, frowning, trying to equate himself with the situation facing him in the next few days. It was dangerous, almost fatal, to be burdened on such a flight with a female. It could be disastrous for her.

She was asleep, her knees curled up beneath her chin, the blanket pulled around her shoulders. He stood in the failing light, watching her for long moments. She seemed incredibly young. She breathed like an infant, her hair pushed back, her lips slightly parted. There was a deep peace in her as she lay there defenseless, exposed. He began to dislike himself for stirrings deep inside.

He busied himself unwrapping the bundle of food Milton had provided from the Margate restaurant. There was bread and cheese and cold meat and a bottle of red

111

wine—homemade, he saw. He selected enough to give them strength for another day and parceled it out on part of the paper wrappings. He sat cross-legged, munching, sipping. The evening song of birds came to him from the pines, small animals rustled in the undergrowth. The horses grazed, moving hesitantly in their hobbles. He had to picket the bay, he knew, but Star would stand under any conditions.

Doc Reynolds' bay, he thought, what a horse laugh that was. Stolen, at that. They could be hanged for it if the wrong people caught them. If the Eggerlys pushed hard enough, there could be trouble at Fort Apache. General Carr was a stern one, not like good old Crook with his canvas jacket and pants and his mule and his patience and knowledge of whites and Indians of the frontier. Crook was in Wyoming, chasing Sioux, and Carr was trying, with little experience, to deal with the Apaches.

Well, no man excepting Crook could handle the Apache. The little savages of the mountains and desert were an odd breed, as Carney knew full well. They had quirks in their nature beyond the ken of the white settlers. They never forgot a friend or an enemy and they took revenge for their wrongs, fancied or real, upon whoever was closest. They drank a good deal of tiswin in certain seasons and when drunk, they were even more mysterious and untrustworthy. As Crook had said, they hated each other most of the time, and hundreds of them even now were acting as scouts for the troopers against their own people.

The girl's eyes opened, she started, sat up straight, staring around. She saw Carney, and the planes of her face altered, she smiled. The last rays of the sun struck across her and made her beautiful.

She said, "I feel better already. Is that food?"

"It ain't hay," he assured her, offering a sandwich.

"Thank you." She began eating without delay, neatly, hungrily disposing of the bread, meat, and cheese. She reached for the wine bottle and took a healthy swig. She asked, "Have we come far enough?"

"I think so."

"Do we stay here for the night?"

"I believe so." He swallowed and went on. "If they were coming down the road, they'd have been here by now. I covered our tracks where we left it. I got a hunch Shriver will delay 'em, he's a sly one. Only thing to worry about now is Apaches."

"Fireboy?"

"They call him that. They don't know what a medicine man can do to a tribe of Indians. How they get to believe because they want to, because it means us whites have got to be beaten and chased away."

She thought about that, finishing her sandwich, drinking the last of the wine. "I wonder what it would be like to be an Indian? Your land gone, troops chasing you, all your rights and beliefs taken away. That wouldn't be good."

"You'd hate pretty good," he said. "You'd never get it through your head that it can really happen. That's how come a medicine man can get 'em roused up to tackle a whole town like Sautelle. They just can't believe they won't get it all back."

"They might have been sorry later on, but they'd have lynched us back in Sautelle, wouldn't they? White people, they'd have shot us or hanged us. Wouldn't they?"

"There wasn't time to wait and see," he said drily.

"They might have been sorry later on, but they'd have done it," she averred positively. "You could feel it in the air."

"Maybe so. Maybe not. There are some good people in the town."

"You think I'd have been safe to take the stage," she said. "You think Fuller would have got me away."

"Like I say, there wasn't time to chance it." He knew he would be better off without her, with Fuller and the five hundred dollars as her shield, but he was not going to make her feel a burden. She had too much courage, he could not let her down. "We'll get to Fort Apache, and then you'll be all right."

"You think so?" She lay back on her blanket, her face turned away from him. She picked at the food he gave her.

113

"I got an old friend there, knew him all my life. Sergeant John. Once I lived on a post, when I was a button. He'll have some ideas."

"You lived on an Army Post?"

"I lived anywhere they'd have me until I could rope a calf," he said briefly. He had never told his entire story to anyone and had no intention of starting now. It was a shameful past, he always thought—no family, nothing that belonged to him, just a succession of people who were stuck with him.

She seemed to have lost interest. She was burrowing into the blanket, twisting her neck. "It's getting cold."

"It'll be worse before morning." He went to the bedrolls and unwrapped them. He threw her two blankets and a slicker, in case a wind came up to sweep the mesa.

"If you dig into the base of the tree, it'll help. Keep to the south side. It's a good idea if you can sleep some now. We'll be startin' for the fort at daybreak."

She said, "I feel like I could sleep for two days."

"Good, that's fine." He went restlessly back to the pine tree. From its base he could see below them into a meadow. The false spring had brought out wildflowers that now had no color, lacking the sunlight. He was still curious about the motion he may or may not have detected in the oak grove. He was far from the Apaches in acuteness, but he knew their ways as well as any white man could and he was wary of them as few white men would be.

The girl was rolled up like a cocoon now, back asleep, oblivious to the world. He arranged his own blankets but was unable to descend into them, his mind whirring like the tail of a rattler. Things had happened too fast since Tombstone. He felt as though he were running behind himself, trying to catch up. He finally dragged one of his blankets around his shoulders and sat hunched on the brim of the mesa, staring at nothing.

Thus he saw Nok-e-da-klinne and his band when they finally decided it was safe to form upon the breast of the meadow and build their fire. He was astounded

114

that they had not scouted the mesa. Then he knew that he had covered his tracks so well that for once he had fooled them and that there was no other road up to the summit, where he sat and watched. Nor was there any other road down, he remembered. If they detected him now, if one of the horses betrayed them or the girl started up in her sleep, crying out, this would be the end.

He was a good distance away from them, but he moved stealthily, rolling over, crawling back so that even in dusk he might not be skylined. He divested himself of the blanket and carried it to the bay horse, removing the hobbles, holding the horse by the nose, the blanket ready to drape over its head. He led the animal far to the other side of the mesa and tethered it to a sapling. When he returned, Betsy was awake, her eyes white in the accumulating darkness. He put a finger to his lips but instantly knew she was aware of something untoward and was silently squirreling out of the blankets.

He went close and whispered in her ear, "Wait here. Not a sound, don't even scrape your boot."

She nodded as he took Star away, and he was struck with her instant recognition of the situation. He brought his rifle back with him this trip and extra ammunition. He saw her huddled beneath the pine tree and took a deep breath of the high, thin air. If they got through this night, they would be the luckiest people in Arizona.

She moved very close to him, and he motioned her to creep cautiously in his wake. He made for the spot from where he had first seen the Apaches. They had a fire going, and he could hear the voice of Nok-e-da-klinne faintly on the breeze that had sprung up. The girl shivered, and he pressed her arm, grateful for the favoring wind blowing away from the Indians.

"If they don't send a scout up here, we're all right for a while," he said into her ear.

"They're dancing," she said. The fire had been built for illumination, he could see. They were already moving in a circle, shuffling, not yet worked up to the heights.

"He's making medicine. He's got to get them believing again."

115

"Believing what?"

"That he can bring the dead back to life."

"They believe that?"

"They believe anything he says right now." There was a stir, and he saw a body being brought from among them and laid beside the fire, unstirring. It might be one of those from the raid, one he had shot down. Nok-e-da-klinne poised beside it, and the dancing feet picked up speed as torsos bent, straightened, bent, straightened, and the moccasined feet drummed in unison. They were not really good dancers, but they had an instinctive rhythm. It seemed as though he could reach down and touch them, so clear was the night.

The medicine man took dust from a small leather pouch and ran it through his fingers, allowing the breeze to waft it across the prone figure. His high voice keened a ritual of his own making. Carney could understand the words, "Oh, Great Spirit, I call upon you, call upon you, call upon you. It is the time of your people, you have promised. I, Nok-e-da-klinne, demand that you raise up the brother who lays here before you . . ."

There was a lot more to it, mainly guff, Carney thought. This was no ancient rite, this was nothing he remembered from the scanty lore of the tough, hard-bitten little Apaches of the south. This medicine man was a bit crazy, perhaps, a small man, older than the others, wrinkled bent-back, ugly, but with a dignity that he used in his performance to great advantage.

Betsy asked, "What is he saying?"

He told her, adding, "He's got the nerve of the devil, trying to bring that corpus back to life. But if he fails, he'll blame it on the white people. He'll moan and cry that we've interfered with his work. I got an idea he's aimin' to head back to Cibicu and pick up more braves. I got a hunch he ain't feelin' so powerful since Sautelle. But he's a canny one. Just don't make a sound, even at this distance. Sometimes I think they got an extra sense that's left out of us."

She said, "He's working up to something big, all right. He's really got them going."

Nok-e-da-klinne was beating out a tempo with a

116

long eagle's feather stained bright red to match his headband. He was naked except for a breechclout. The others wore their high moccasins and their leggins, but the medicine man worked close to the skin. Suddenly he began flicking at the body by the fire with the feather.

Screams arose now. The dancing grew more furious, the cries were demanding. These people were not supplicating, they were angrily insisting that their god restore life to the departed, Carney realized.

Still, the body of the prone Apache did not stir. Nok-e-da-klinne turned his face to the skies and raised the scarlet feather, brandishing it. Instinctively Carney lifted his eyes.

Unnoticed by any but the medicine man, heavy clouds had drifted down from the mountain peaks. A drop of rain fell on Carney's chin. Before he could drag the girl back, the sky lit up as it could in that country, white as day, bright as the sunshine. Betsy flinched, burying her head, shuddering as thunder hammered a roar that shook the world.

Carney said, "The horses. Get the horses."

She was scared, but she put down her head and ran as raindrops big as saucers pelted down. Carney levered the rifle, grimly staring down into blackness as Nok-e-da-klinne barked orders, scattering the fire. There was no question about it, the Apaches had spotted them. They had been skylined only for the lightning flash, but it was enough.

He held the muzzle of the gun on the only path that led up to the mesa. They would be scrambling, welcoming the rain, coming in their way, like snakes in the dark. He heard Betsy talking to the frightened ponies as she led them to the bedrolls, knew she was packing quickly as possible. There was no target, there was nothing to do but take the risk that came immediately to mind.

He retreated, keeping his eyes on the narrow path. She had the bedrolls ready. He cinched them, drew a deep breath, and said, "We're going to run through 'em."

She nodded, close enough for him to hear her breathing. "They saw us."

117

"They saw us."

"We're to ride through them?"

"You put that bay on my heels and come down lick-ety-split," he told her. "We'll get through."

"Will we?"

"It's dark. They won't expect us," he told her with a confidence he did not feel. "When we hit the main road, we'll head for Fort Apache. Understand?"

"Fort Apache," she repeated. Her teeth were chattering, but she was able to swing into the saddle, although she winced at the pain in her overworked muscles.

"If we get separated, go to Sergeant John Smith. You can't forget that name, John Smith."

"I'll remember," she said.

"Have you got the derringer?"

"I've got it. They won't take me alive," she said, her voice growing stronger.

"Best we should get started before they can think." He mounted. "All right?"

She said, "Go ahead, Will. I'll follow you. I'll . . . I'll follow you anywhere."

He could not see her face in the dark. He ducked his shoulders, feeling the impact of her words, hearing the way she pronounced them. Then he struck spurs into the surprised Star and went hurtling down the hill, rifle in his hand, a prayer deep in his heart.

Chapter Twelve

THE RAIN WAS thick as sheets of glass, and the path was steep down the mountainside, but the worst of it was that Carney could not see the girl and how she was making it. He wanted the black Star in the lead because he had confidence in the horse and he did not know the bay upon which Betsy Gaye rode. Further, knowing the Apaches, he wanted to be in the van if they came up in

118

the blackness to grab the lead horse. Yet he worried as they crashed and careened, all sense of direction and balance gone, and the thunder pealed around their heads.

Once there was lightning, and he thought he saw a dark face and the gleam of a gun barrel. He fired offhand but never knew if he scored a hit. He let Star have his head and rode low in the saddle, straining his eyes, his ears, every nerve.

He had never been aware of this sort of tension before. He had ridden through many a tight without thinking about it much, one way or another. It was the girl, of course, and he should resent it.

But he did not. He only worried.

The black horse stumbled and almost went down. He held tight, bringing up the strong jaw, and the reliable and gallant animal recovered in a flash. Once he thought he had lost the bay when a shot sounded. He craned back, and there they came, girl and pony, right on the button, scrambling down the path.

The lightning obliged with a short burst, and he could see her face, set and determined. Then they were skidding down into a gulley already running with the threat of flash flood. Star went up the other side, his haunches quivering with the strain, and the bay pony followed.

Shots sounded, and once a bullet came very close to Carney's skull. He did not return the fire, preferring the cloak of darkness as they spun eastward on a road that wound up and up through the pass and then down on the trail to Fort Apache, running free.

It had all been very swift, and he knew there were Apaches still following. He checked Star until the girl could come up alongside, then let the horses blow.

"It ain't over," he called.

"I know." Her voice was strong if not quite calm.

"If your pony's got the bottom, we may be able to outrun them."

"It's a good horse," she told him. "I'm ready."

"You go on ahead now," he ordered.

"All right."

They began the steady run. Behind them he could hear the sound of pursuit, but he was thinking about the trail to Cibicu up ahead and wondering if Nok-e-da-klinne wasn't also debating that turnoff. In Carney's mind it became the goal, the point they must make with a good lead over the Apaches. He set Star to it as the rain settled into a steady, slashing downpour.

There was also further danger of flash flood. There were places where the water came down the gorges and ran across the road through sudden dips. Many an unwary rider had lost his life in these freakish floods. Alone on Star he would not have worried, but the bay, however sturdy, was a smaller beast and not nearly so fast.

In fact, there were faster horses behind them, his ear told him. Above the pelting of the rain he heard the sound of them coming up. The Apaches had stolen some very fine stock along their way. He pulled the rifle from under its protective tarp and reined in.

Betsy Gaye said, "What is it?"

"Just ride," he said impatiently. "You can't lose us. Ride!"

She knew that Fort Apache lay ahead. She hesitated only one moment, then obeyed. It occurred to him, waiting in the rain and the darkness, that a lesser woman would have paused for debate. The girl was special, all right.

He had to proceed by his hearing. When two Apache horsemen came flying, he levered the Remington and raised it. They were even with him when he fired the first shot. He heard the scream of a man struck by an unexpected blow, then there was a scrambling and an indistinguishable mass on the road, the sound of horses frightened. Carney held the muzzle low and emptied the chamber into the conglomeration of man and beast and agony.

Then he was astride and riding again. Some of the fear of the enemy had inoculated Star, and they flew along the road to Fort Apache.

He heard the rush of water before he came up to the girl on the bay pony. Star snuffled and skidded in slimy soil. If there was close pursuit now, Carney could not hear it over the sound of the flash flood.

120

Betsy Gaye said, "I heard the shots."

"Never got out of a tight without a killin', not yet."

"Don't think about that." Her voice was urgent, soft yet firm.

"Don't worry. Head upstream aways. We got to cross, there's no other way. They'll catch us if we don't cross."

"Yes. I thought so."

"You better follow me. That horse of yours is good at followin'."

"Yes," she said.

He could not see her. The rain pelted them, so that there was not a dry stitch on their bodies. He could feel it squishing in his boots, and this even now made him impatient and angry because he was very conscious of his footwear, and if he could not give attention to it, even the fine glove leather would deteriorate. He sent Star up the side of the slope to the south of the road.

It was a quarter mile before he found a possible spot of departure. The girl sat alongside him, wordless. They looked at the raging stream, at the swirling branches of small trees uprooted and sent pell-mell to a far destination, barely discernible in the darkness. They listened to the dangerous sound of the water.

"Stay close," he said. "If you can, that is."

"I'll try."

He could detect no fear in her voice. She seemed to have full confidence that he could get anything done, pull them through any crisis. Just like a dam-fool woman, he thought. He loosened the bridles of the horses.

On the instant he realized how unfair he was being. She had performed, she had not merely followed. She had done everything asked of her and more, far more.

He said in a different tone, "This is a matter of luck, I promise you. Just plain dumb luck. If we don't get hit by a rock or somethin', if we come out near the road, it'll be luck."

She said, "I know about flash floods."

"Okay, then. You ready?"

"It's better than Apaches," she said, and actually laughed.

They rode into the water. The force of the current

121

was astounding. They spun around twice before they could get their breaths. The downpour did not abate one whit, it did seem their luck was finally out. The two horses, fighting with bridles free, heads up, clashed together, he could feel her leg against his, thought that broken bones might end it all, whether or not they got across.

He reached out and held her firmly, and then they were apart again, and he felt foolish because there was nothing he could have done had she been thrown loose. Star kicked, and a thorny bush swirled at them and away.

There was nothing to do but sit. He thought about a thousand things as the horses swam and the current eddied. The night seemed endless, the storm a part of eternity. He lost the girl on the bay completely, Star almost went under. He thought it was over, that here was an inglorious end indeed, the end of a gunslinger, drowned in a mountain flood, a matter for laughter around the rude frontier saloons. And the Eggerlys would feel cheated, at least Simon Eggerly would. Another bush slashed at him, and he wondered how far below the road they had been swept by now.

Then the girl called out clearly, and he grabbed at a stinging, wet branch. It held. His thighs ached with cramping, but Star came around, swimming hard. Then there was footing.

A step, two steps. Star went under, and Carney took water in his collar. The girl called again, and he saw her on dry land, reaching out to him. He grabbed and caught hold of a vine of some sort, and Star came blowing and snorting and scrambling, finding footing in some miraculous manner that drew them up. They came out, shaking water like dogs coming out of a pond.

She said, "As you said, plain luck. The pony found the way, then you came right into it."

He looked for the road, saw it not a hundred yards away. He said, "Is the rain stoppin', or do I just imagine it?"

"I think it's slacking off."

"We'll ride. It'll keep us warm to ride."

122

"I'll never be warm again." Her teeth were chattering, but her voice was cheerful.

"We'll make a camp. I know a place." He remembered a cabin between here and Fort Apache. The girl would rather freshen up, he sensed, before arriving among the military. They needed a rest, time to recuperate.

"The Apaches?"

"They may come on. Most likely not."

"But shouldn't we make for the fort?"

"No, I wouldn't say so. Got to clean up some. The fort's a rough place. This cabin, it's high and dry."

Now they rode in silence. She had voiced one opinion, and he had clamped down hard on her. There was nothing more to say for this time. They rode, and the rain again increased, blowing in freakish fashion. The storm clouds had bounced off the mountain peaks and remained, glowering and emptying their contents over the countryside.

That they found the trail quickly was due to a pine he remembered, a lonely stick of a tree growing out of rock, stubborn. He turned off, and the girl perforce followed, winding up a narrow ascent, coming around a rocky turn, suddenly almost ramming into the dark mass of the log cabin.

There was a leanto where they could tether the horses out of the wet. The roof leaked, but it was comparative comfort for the steaming animals. Carney went to the side door and found it unlatched.

They entered, and from deep within his bedroll he produced wax matches and sandpaper upon which to scratch them. In the fireplace were the remnants of old newspapers, calendars, an almanac, neatly laid. The baffle had prevented seepage, a New England man had constructed this chimney not too many years ago. There was a box containing sticks of mesquite, which burned merrily.

It was one room, adobe, thick walls, double bunks, one narrow window, one high window, a sink but no pump. The mountain stream, a trickle in normal weather,

123

roared nearby, flowing northward. It was all as Carney remembered. He turned to the girl.

She was forlorn, facing the fireplace, her hair hanging dank along the planes of her face, the slanted eyes hooded, somber. Her skin was pale, there were dark circles in the hollows, her hands shook just a little as she plucked at her soaking wet garments.

He felt a deep twinge of pity and shame. "Didn't mean to be short with you. I got a notion about Noke-da-klinne. I got a notion he lost too many men. He's supposed to bring 'em back to life, and it ain't workin' so good. The old man's too smart to stick with a bunch that's got to begin to wonder. The road to Cibicu is just short of that flash flood. Why should he cross it? He'd figure me to hole up if things got hot. Then he'd lose more people and he can't afford that."

Her face lightened. "Oh, I see."

"Didn't have time to go into all that," he apologized. It was the longest explanation he had given anyone about anything in his mature life.

"I should have known," she murmured. "I guess I'm just not gaited to a night like this."

Now he was really stung. He blurted, "My Gawd, gal, who is? You done real good. I don't see how you ever did so good."

She said humbly, "But I'm beat now, Will. I'm dead beat."

He drew a deep breath, then said roughly, "There's enough wood to keep the fire goin'. I'll see to the horses and check the road."

"I'm sorry," she said. "I'm so cold . . ."

He laid out the bedroll. The oilskin cover had kept the blankets dry at the middle. He reached into his saddlebag and took out his soft rag and oilcan and wiped the Remington dry and clean with practiced hands. He reloaded with ammunition from a sequestered box.

"Use anything you need," he told her. "I'll knock when I get back."

He pulled his hat down over his dripping nose and went back into the driving rain. He wiped down the horses and covered them as best he could with a split tarpau-

124

lin. Then he walked back down the path to a spot where he could dimly see the road below. In his mind a time clock measured minutes and quarter hours.

If the Apaches had crossed the flash flood, they would be here within the next thirty minutes or so, is the way it came out. He had never been without the thought, it had persisted when he had made the decision to pause for a rest before making the ride to Fort Apache. If they did cross, there were two alternatives, either they would know about the cabin and investigate or they would be ignorant of its existence and continue the chase on the road. It was his considered opinion that Nok-e-da-klinne would not risk further losses.

He hunkered down beneath a dripping bush and waited. He thought about the girl in the cabin. She would be changing clothes now, dry and comfortable. She would be so weary that she might even sleep, if she could clean up the accumulated dirt of the cabin.

He found himself wishing she would be asleep when he returned to the cabin. If this was not normal, he could not help it, he thought wearily, the days had been too swift and the nights too long. His eyelids were heavy, and his spirit within him was flickering low. There had been too many killings again.

Even the Apaches, he thought, they had a right to live. They killed because it was their nature and because the white man had never given them a reason to do otherwise. Nok-e-da-klinne was probably a bit crazy, but he was trying in his way to lead his people back to their natural way of life. The reservation at Cibicu was no haven for people like the Apache.

And Sautelle, where for a fleeting moment he had thought he might find a home, there had been killing in that town. Maybe some small good had come to the Margates—just maybe, because the woman was hard hit and Carney had seen such wounds before, all having ill results. But what of Marshal Shriver, what had he to hope for? And the Eggerlys were present and in force, and Simon would be among them, on Carney's trail, whipping them to action.

No, Sautelle was a thing of the past, like so many

other places. No matter which way he turned, which side he was on, there was a call upon his gun. It was a thing that happened to a man, no use to complain. It had happened to others in this country, and they did what they must, they went on until someone drew faster or got behind them in the dark, or waylaid them with a long gun. It was part of the West, and he knew better than to swim against the tide. He had seen men hang up their guns to escape it—and be murdered.

It was no life for a woman to share, that was for sure.

The rain beat down, and he squatted beneath his poncho, wet and uncomfortable. No one came down the road from Sautelle, no one came up the road from Fort Apache. The time he had set in his mind elapsed. He arose, his joints stiff, every bone crying for surcease in slumber. He plodded back to the cabin.

Light shone through the window. The fire would be dying now, but it would be enough. He wanted only to lie down and forget everything for a few hours.

Before he could knock, she had opened the door, causing him to say, "You shouldn't do that. How'd you know it wasn't an Indian?"

She shook her head, retreating, smiling, allowing him to enter. "I was watching."

He stared at her. He had never experienced the recuperative power of womankind, he could not believe what he saw. She had donned a flannel robe that reached from her throat to her ankles, no further, so that her shapely feet in some sort of soft, close-fitting slippers were visible. Her hair was piled atop her head, wrapped in a towel. Her face shone with health and cleanliness. There was an aura of strength and purity that struck at him like a blow. In all his life Will Carney had never seen a woman in this particular aspect, in surroundings that resembled hearth and home.

He had never seen this familiar cabin so resemble a home, either. In the comparatively short time of his vigil she had done remarkable things to the room. She moved to the hearth and tossed some dust into the fire with the aid of a bit of pasteboard, bending, then looking up at him and saying, "You must get out of those clothes at once, Will."

He said, "Yeah," blinking around. She had used the blankets to make up the bunks, she had covered the windows with tarp, which she now secured so that no light could show outside. The puncheon floor was swept of refuse, he could see the stub of an old broom in a corner. Everything was neat and orderly, it reminded him of a barracks under inspection, yet it was subtly different.

She sat on the lower bunk, slanting her eyes at him. "I'm going to turn my back. Take off everything and hang it, you see?"

He saw her own clothing, stretched on his rope, far enough from the fire to let them dry slowly. He batted his eyes at underthings fringed with lace, took off his hat, deposited it a careful distance from the flames. "There's some more wood in the shed, I noticed. I'll get it."

He went out where the two horses steamed, nickering at him. He was slightly dizzy for a moment. He picked up an armful of the wood and went back into the cabin. She was curled up in the bunk, her face to the wall. Was she, then, asleep already?

He put down the wood and began to get out of his wet clothing. Twice he hesitated, worried lest she turn over in her sleep. When he was stripped, he grabbed a shirt and dried himself, then got into clean, dry long drawers and shirt. He refurbished the fire, enough to hold for a while, got out his bottle of glycerine and rubbed his hands slowly and with great care. After a moment he was aware of her gaze.

He made a motion to cover himself, but she shook her head, smiling. "Your boots. Will they be all right?"

"These are kind of new," he said. He picked them up, drying them, using the glycerine on them. "You know about good leather, huh?"

"I'm a ranch girl," she reminded him. "I noticed your boots back in Tombstone. Nice."

He felt more at ease because of her offhand manner. "You notice things pretty good, don't you?"

"And you? I suppose you don't see everything around?"

"Yeah," he said. "It's a habit you get into if you're a man like me."

"Hoooo," she said. "A man like you? What kind of a man do you think you are, Will Carney?"

"Just as soon not get into that." He lowered his head, working on the boots. "Reckon you better get some sleep, Betsy. Tomorrow may be a hard day."

"Apaches?"

"No, I don't reckon on them. But there's always somethin'. Eggerlys or somethin'."

"You think the Eggerlys will be after us from Sautelle?"

"I don't know. But I know Simon Eggerly wants hunk for his pet son, Bud. And he don't ever give up. If I can get you to the fort, you'll be out of it, at least."

She dropped her head back, closing her eyes. "I see."

"I've been thinkin'. There's this ranchero in Mantocloz. Riley, he wants me down there."

"It's a thought." Her voice was low.

"If I can get across the border, that might be the best way to go. I'll tell you plain, I'm gettin' sick of all the killin'. Wherever I go, somebody dies." He raised his volume unconsciously. "Not that I take all the blame. I don't go for violence. I don't think it's in me, never did. But some people, things happen around them. Things just plain happen."

"I've noticed that, too. Around me, too."

That gave him pause. He thought back to Bud Eggerly and all that had transpired since. He said wonderingly, "What do you know? That's the truth."

"Yes. Some people are that way."

"Yeah. Didn't think of it before."

She said in a very small voice, "I think I am sleepy now. Will you go to bed, too? Please . . . everything will be all right tonight."

He stood up, looking down at her. She lay with her eyes half-closed, smiling just a little.

He said, "Sure, Betsy . . . sure."

He put down his boots and wiped his hands. She

128

was so thoroughly natural, like a child, but that wasn't any child beneath that blanket. That was a whole lot of woman. He knew it, every drop of his blood knew it. Why didn't he want to do something about it, right now?

She liked him, he knew that. She had a real tender feeling for him. She had risked her life, she had followed through every step of the way. Why was he stepping up into that top bunk? It plain wasn't natural, he thought. It sure wasn't like Will Carney.

He couldn't find an answer that early morning. He was so utterly weary that he didn't even think about being hungry. It was warm and comfortable in the cabin, in the bunk he remembered from the past . . . he did not want to recall what had happened here, in this place in that time.

He fell asleep just before the false dawn of the mountains broke through the clouds to clear away the last of the rain.

Chapter Thirteen

IN SAUTELLE the weather had turned warm, and the sun shone. Simon Eggerly sat in the lobby of the hotel and talked in his heaviest manner.

"You people got to understand, this is for your own good. There can only be one way to go—grab and hold on and make everyone prosper. It takes a boss, and I'm the boss."

Margate listened from behind the desk. His wife could hear, lying in the bedroom. Cousin Sim Martin from Tucson was there, although he had no proper jurisdiction this far north. Bo, Peter, and Jack Eggerly from the Sautelle area were together in a group nearest the door, twiddling their hats, not looking directly at their relative from the South. Marshal Dan Shriver was close to the stairway, perspiring, silent.

Paul Eggerly stood in a corner. The hulking second son's blond hair was cut short, giving him the appearance of a slightly stupid ox, his face was set in heavy planes that showed no emotion.

The big man went on, "When somebody does wrong to the boss, everybody turns to and helps. The Governor ain't goin' to interfere, the Army don't know nothin' about it and don't care. It's up to us, the people." He grinned, resembling a grizzly bear, abjuring them. "You all know me. I aim to get Carney and hang him."

Bo Eggerly made bold to remark, "I was you, Simon, I'd bushwhack him. It's a heap safer."

"Hangin' for a murderer," pronounced Simon. "He called the turn when he murdered Bud."

Paul moved then, and Simon fixed angry eyes on him.

"You, Paul. You'll do the job. You'll be your brother's killer's executioner. I got it all planned."

Paul did not respond.

"Now that it's all understood," said Simon. "Whereats that Mex of yourn, Sim?"

"Comin' down the street, lickety-split," said Jack Eggerly from the doorway.

Simon arose and strode forward. "Now we'll larn somethin'. Everybody get ready to ride."

Sanchez dismounted and tied up to the rack as the Eggerlys came out to him. He stood there, removing his hat, the sun shining on his glossy black hair, and shook his head.

"Flash floods. It will take a day or so, no? The roads, they are out."

"We'll go cross-country," roared Simon.

"Not possible," Sanchez replied.

Bo Eggerly asked, "You see Apache sign?"

"None. They are in the hills or they are gone to reservation," Sanchez said positively. "One day, two day, we find Carney. And the lady. Oh, yes, we find them, Señor Eggerly." He stared at the big man. "I promise you faithful. We find them."

"You got the right spirit, Sanchez," said Simon. "More'n some of my own kin, I can see that. Oh, I can see it. A two-bit gunslinger comes in, he scares hell outa you. You leave him to the Injuns, sure, you do—you, Bo, and Jack and all of you. Let Fireboy take care of him. You ain't got the guts to go after him your own selves. By God and by damn, I'm goin' to go after him. And I'm goin' to hang him slow and easy. I'm goin' to choke the life outa him inch by inch, breath by breath. I'm goin' to stand there and watch and I'm goin' to enjoy. I'll show him and the whole country what happens when you mess with Eggerlys."

He stumped down off the verandah and across the street to the restaurant. They straggled after him, the men who had followed him from the South.

Bo and Peter and Jack Eggerly and the cousins hung back. Margate came from the hotel and stood unnoticed in the background. Dan Shriver drifted near.

Bo Eggerly said, "Well, boys. Two days or so, my stock needs tendin'."

"Got work after the rain," agreed Jack.

There was a moment's silence, then they began moving toward the livery stable. Across the street Milton was rushing around trying to serve Simon and Paul and the others. Margate looked at the Sautelle town marshal.

Shriver said, "Best keep out of it. Can't stop Simon from hangin' Carney. Might's well stay quiet."

Margate said, "You really think Carney will hang?"

"Why, no, come to think of it. Ole Carney, he'll never surrender agin. Ole Carney, he'll hole up and shoot a passel of 'em. But they'll get him in the end. Too many of 'em."

Margate sighed. "I expect you're right, Shriver. There are too many of them."

"Kinda hate the thought, my own self," muttered Shriver. "Way he grabbed my kid and ran and brought him safe. He ain't the worst man ever hit Sautelle."

"No, he isn't," agreed Margate. "You'll ride with Simon? You'll watch Carney die?"

"Got no choice," said the marshal. "Trouble with me is, I'm a man is always owned. All my life. It ain't a nice way to be, Margate. Nope. It ain't nice a-tall." He rubbed his mouth with a thumb, turned, and went across the street and entered the restaurant with the rest of the Eggerly contingent.

Margate wandered into his wife's bedroom. She was awake, and her fever had abated. He sat beside her.

She said, "He's a bad man, that Simon Eggerly."

"He's made of the stuff of tyrants."

"Will he hang Carney?"

"If he can get the rope around Carney's neck."

"Yes. He would do it." She looked out of the window. "Charles?"

"Yes, dear?"

"I wish we could do something."

"Yes. I do, too."

After a moment she said, "He gave us the ability to hope."

"We will hope." Margate could walk with only one cane. He found himself much stronger. But he was, he knew, incapable of an act that might aid Carney. "I'm sorry, dear. I can do nothing but hope."

She reached out her hand, contrite. "It is wonderful that we have that much, Charles. I am happy."

At noon Carney sat upon the promontory and yawned. There was no one in sight, and he knew now that Nok-e-da-klinne had not pursued them. The flash flood would not subside for that day, not until night at any rate, probably not then after such a ferocious storm. They could go to Fort Apache at their leisure, and he could leave Betsy in safe hands.

He pondered on that morning and how she had been up before him and had made coffee in the fireplace. By then he was watching her in her long, soft robe. He had seen how carefully she toasted the stale bread for their breakfast, making it tasty with melted cheese from their scanty rations. It was a new and rather wonderful experience for him.

Then she had gone to the window and put aside the tarp, not taking it down, arranging it like a curtain, a poor sort of curtain but better than the bare, staring square opening in the log wall. And the sun had struck through her gown for a moment, so that he could not help staring, with every line of her body silhouetted, nothing concealed in the bright glow.

And he had quickly closed his eyes. Why? He could not imagine the reason. No experience had prepared him for his emotion, this odd forbearance.

A moment later he had been rewarded when her face came close and she whispered, "Awake, Will?"

It was a lovely face, and he had dissembled and asked, "How long you been up? Yeah . . . I'm awake now."

She had served him, and no meal had ever tasted so good in his life before. Their conversation had been sparse, but they had smiled often upon one another, as if each recognized there were things between them deeply understood.

But now he understood not at all, he admitted to himself. He arose and trailed his rifle, starting back to the cabin. They would simply move on, get to the fort, and take leave of one another, that was all there was to it. He hoped she had put those borrowed pants on again by the time he got back.

Then he heard the unmistakable sound of horses approaching from the east. He swung around with the rifle like an animal at bay before he realized that he recognized the sound, that this was a group of the military. He ran back to the hilltop and saw them, two troops of 6th Cavalry. He called out, and Sergeant Smith responded, went to the officer in charge, saluted, reported, then dismounted and climbed up to where Carney waited, a round-faced, tough veteran with wide-spaced, merry blue eyes.

"Carney, what you doin' here?" They shook hands. "You oughta get the hell outa this country. The wires have been burnin' about you."

"Simon Eggerly?"

"Matter of fact, a fella named Margate. You know him?"

"I know him."

"Sent a telegraph message to you. Eggerly's in Sautelle with a bunch. Got a rope greased for you."

133

"That figures."

"You headin' for the fort?"

"Sort of." He hesitated, then knew he must confide in his old friend. "Got a lady with me."

"Oh-ho! Good ole Carney."

"Good old nothin'. I want her safe at the fort. I want you to look out for her."

"Now, that's plumb nice of you, ole friend."

"Nothin' like that, I tell you. She's a lady."

Sergeant Smith sobered. "I see . . . that's different. But we're headin' for Cibicu right now."

"Nok-e-da-klinne?"

"Yeah. General Carr got a bug up his butt. And we got Cruse and his Apache scouts comin' up. I don't like it nohow."

Carney debated a moment with himself, then asked, "How about we pick you up on the way back?"

"If Simon Eggerly don't get you first?"

"He won't. There's a flash flood ahead. You skip it, but he'd have to cross it."

"Then you might pick us up on the creek. Captain won't say 'no' if there's a lady along."

"Tomorrow evenin'?"

"Right . . . You seen Nocky-boy?"

"Had a little thing with him. He don't like me none. He lost a few braves. I figured he'd go back to Cibicu."

"Lost some, huh? That's bad. Uglies them up to lose people." Smith turned away to where the company was growing restive. "Well, see you mañana."

"Watch out for them. The old man's got 'em believin'."

"Tell it to the Captain. Name o' Hentig. Not a bad one, not a good one, neither." Smith made a face and slid down the hill on the heels of his boots.

Carney watched the troops out of sight, then the scouts came straggling along, talking among themselves in their own language. He recognized Mosby, a squat, pockmarked Apache whom he had never trusted. There was unease among them, and he did not like it at all. Indian medicine is powerful to all Indians, friendlies or

134

not, he thought, going up to the cabin in the clearing upon the hilltop.

Betsy was not inside the cabin, and he felt a ridiculous moment of panic . . . where could she go from here? He looked down toward the swollen creek, and there she was, on her knees. He wondered what she was doing and went down to investigate.

She looked up, face flushed from exertion. She had a piece of soap in her wet hand. "Your shirts. And all our wet underclothing was soiled."

He saw the garments hanging on a stunted dead tree. "You expect that to dry before we leave?"

"The sun is hot enough. It's such a beautiful day." She was wearing a loose gingham dress. "I hated to put those dirty pants on again. Do we have to leave so soon?"

"Matter of fact, we don't." He told her about the troop and his plan to ride safely with it to the fort.

"Oh, that's wonderful, to have a day to rest and clean up." She was radiant.

"There's not much food, but we can pick 'em up tomorrow night on Cibicu Creek, the man said. If you don't mind goin' hungry a few hours."

"We can make do," she told him. "There are ways of stretching vittles." She stretched her arms toward the sky. "The wonderful sunshine. Why, we could take a swim in the creek."

He squinted at the swift-running water. "Truth to tell, I ain't that good a swimmer."

"Well, we can just sit around and be comfortable. It seems years since we could do just that." She was off toward the cabin.

He stood a moment as another memory struck him. When he had been here before, there was a man named Jackson, a crook and a killer who had murdered his partner. It was here that Carney had cornered him and shot him. Jackson was buried on the other side of the hill. Violence, wherever Carney went, violence here where the sun did not now seem so bright. He looked again at the washing she had done for him, shaking his head. He

135

slowly plodded toward the cabin, feeling old and weary and somehow lost.

She was arranging things around the room, although they had seemed very well distributed before. She was humming a tune.

He said, "I remember that one. You were singin' it the night Bud Eggerly went at you."

"Never mind Bud Eggerly," she said.

"I don't mind him," he said sharply.

She stopped what she was doing, coming to him, her eyes concerned. "Ah, Will, but you do, I know you do. You mind all of them. I didn't mean it that way. Don't be hard with me. I just meant to forget everything for today, our day."

"Why, sure," he said awkwardly, taken aback at her show of feeling. "All right."

"We can loaf around and do nothing. After a while we can take in the wash. Then we'll eat a little. Then maybe we can just sit in the sun."

"Anything you say."

"Then I can have today? For us?"

"Why, sure." He was not quite certain of the implication, but he realized he could not at this moment refuse her anything.

"And can we talk? Like people? Only more so, telling the truth to each other? Can we do that?"

"It ain't an easy thing." It had always been most difficult for him to explain anything about himself to anybody, he knew he was not good at it. "We could try."

She was excited in a bright, open manner, like a child. "Let's eat a bite right now. Then we can take a little walk, maybe. It'll work out. I'm good at it, talking . . . and listening."

"Anything you say is all right."

She moved with grace in her pretty dress. He found he could scarcely take his eyes from her. They ate a thin sandwich out of doors, watching the horses forage where he had tethered them in the green that grew near the creek. She began to tell him about her early life in East Texas, and although there was nothing exciting about the recital, he found himself hanging on every word.

136

All the harrowing experiences she had suffered had obviously begun with their meeting in Tombstone and the death of Bud Eggerly.

Also, it seemed that there had been no men in her life. Or if there were a male name somewhere along the line, it was dismissed with a lift of the lip and a toss of the head. Carney did not really note this, he was merely unconsciously relieved that it had been that way. What he did notice was the way she moved in the sunlight, especially within the cabin, touching this and that, making everything seem warm and right and . . . homelike.

That was something he had never known. The homes he could dimly remember were slovenly and not clean. Everything about Betsy Gaye seemed immaculate, everything shone in her vicinity.

Then she was asking, "But what about you?"

"Me?"

"You must have had some kind of childhood and all."

He shook his head. "Just knockin' around. And livin' with the Apache."

"I don't want to hear about Indians. I want to hear about your life, what you've done, what you've got in mind to do."

He thought for a moment. "Reckon I've just drifted. The kind of man I am, he just drifts."

"No, I mean before that."

"I just don't remember . . . don't know. A man gets a name. Carney . . . fast gun . . . he plays cards. Sometimes he takes a job, deals for the house. He keeps his eye on the door, always sits with his back to the wall." He paused, seeking words. "How'd he get that way? It just happens to some people. He gets along with men like Wyatt and Luke Short and Bat Masterson, they're his kind. They're on the move, too, always on the move. Driftin' is what it is."

"The wash must be dry." She was frowning a little, she had not liked his story. She wanted to think about it, to pursue it properly, so that she might understand and that he, too, might come to know more of himself.

They gathered the clothing carefully, and she folded

137

it neatly, piling it in a bundle on the smooth surface of a large, flat boulder. She sat down against the rock and crossed her slender ankles, showing part of her white, graceful, smooth leg, unaware, preoccupied.

"Tell me, Will, do you have any fun?"

"Fun?" He hadn't thought of that word in many a long year. "You mean . . . women?"

"I know about you and women." She paused, grinned to herself. "That's easy to figure."

"Well, now . . ." he began resentfully, but she interposed.

"I mean, do you like to dance?"

"Ho!"

"You don't ever go to dances?"

He thought of the honky-tonks where you bought the gal a drink and whirled her around to learn if she would make a proper bed companion for the night and said, "People just don't seem to invite me to hoedowns and such. Mostly they're run by church folk."

"You've never been to church?"

"Why, certainly I been to church." The last time had been an Easter in Denver with a religious whore.

"You believe in religion?"

"Well, I guess I don't know exactly what I believe. Churches, they hem me in, all them people and most preachers bein' so mouthy sure of everything. But I reckon there's a God."

"There is a God." She lowered her head, looking at the stream where the turbulence was lessening as the floods subsided. "Yes, there is a God."

"Sure there is. There's plants and trees and animals and bugs and water and air and all kinds of things. Somebody put 'em there, like Somebody put us here."

"Yes. Maybe for a reason." She was solemn.

"Reason or no reason, it figures."

They were silent, agreeing, listening to the flow of the creek over stones, a rippling, pleasing sound. Then she was suddenly bright and gay again, jumping up, running her hands up and down her body, making a face at him.

"I want to swim." She picked up the little piece of

138

soap left over from the washing. "Mainly, I want to get clean all over. A bath. A real bath."

He arose hastily, "That's all right. I got . . . uh . . . things to do."

She was reaching for the buttons on her dress as he went to the cabin. He got out his guns and went over them with minute care and patience. He tended to his cartridges and his gunbelt and holster, making sure all was oiled and supple and ready for use. He thought about the girl. He couldn't get his mind on anything else, and it bothered him.

He remembered he must attend to the horses and was outdoors before he realized she was still swimming in the creek. He went doggedly on, keeping his face averted from that direction. Star and the bay had cropped the green from their staked positions, and he moved them. He was heading back for the cabin feeling somewhat neglected and not understanding that, either, when she called to him and came from behind the large rock, her head bound in a towel, fully dressed and carrying the wash.

"It's so much better than making do with a rag. Best try it, Will. Cold and lovely."

"Maybe you're right about the bath part," he admitted. He rummaged for another bar of soap and watched her trip gaily to the cabin. She was the prettiest thing he had ever seen when she was like that, happy and lighthearted.

He went down to the stream and behind the big rock and stripped and gingerly let himself into the shallows of the creek, huffing and puffing, rubbing his skin with the soap. He even ducked under and gasped and yelled and heard her laughing at him from afar, then leaped out and began toweling himself, chuckling.

She had ways, all right. He had needed a good wash despite the drenching and wiping of the previous night. It took the kinks out of his muscles and out of his mind, too. He felt fully restored as he dressed and went back to the cabin.

She was singing "I dream of Jeannie with the light brown hair . . ." and surprisingly he joined in. To their

139

instant pleasure their voices blended, and they sang it through without missing a note or a word. His baritone was free and well placed, and she patted her hands together and immediately began "Sweet Betsy From Pike," which he also knew, as he remembered so many songs from the saloons, the campfires, the joints in the big cities.

She put the clean clothing away in the careful, useful way that he had begun to know. They kept on singing, enjoying it more and more. The afternoon went away on wings.

He was hoarse when he said in defense of his vocal cords, "We could eat a bit if you can squeeze out anything fit."

She laughed. "I'm good at eking out."

"There's always jerky in my saddlebag, we won't starve."

"I hope we never get to jerky. It's been years, but I never will forget the taste." She bustled, and the time passed swiftly as the mountain air cooled, and it was time to build another fire. They were at ease in each other's company now, she on the lower bunk, he sprawled upon a blanket, the flame flickering as darkness fell, the room safe and comfortable, far from the ever-present dangers of his existence, it seemed to Carney then.

After a long silence, she said, "Will?"

"Yeah?"

"About Mrs. Margate."

He sat up straight. "Mrs. Margate?"

"She was after you there at first."

"You are plumb out of your mind, Betsy."

"See? You didn't notice that time."

He said, "Aw, you're jokin' me. How about you and Farber, huh? How about that?"

"That's not funny," she said severely. "He's dead."

"Mrs. Margate's goin' to be half dead for a long time," he told her.

Again there was stillness in the cabin.

Then he said, "Betsy?"

"Yes?"

140

"What did you mean, you know all about me and women?"

Now it was a giggle. "You're just . . . the way you are."

"And how is that?"

"Oh . . . nice."

"Nice? Who, me?"

"Well, there's two kinds of women, right?"

"I never said so."

"You don't say it. You act it."

"There's more'n two kinds, that's for sure."

"What kind am I?"

"Why, you're a good girl."

She sighed deeply.

He said, "Well, a man can tell."

"What's a good girl, Will?" Her voice was very low, and her face was half hidden in the shadows.

"Well . . . you know. She don't fool around with every Tom, Dick, and Harry."

"Fool around?"

"Well, you know."

"What if a girl who doesn't fool around . . . suddenly feels like she'd like to be fooled around with?"

He wheeled sharply from his contemplation of the fire. "Why, she just gets over it."

"Unless she's in love?"

"Unless she's in . . ." He broke off, and now the silence was like a blanket over the cabin.

Then she whispered, "Will, why don't you come over here and talk with me?"

"No," he said flatly.

"Why not?"

"Because."

"Because I'm a good girl?"

"You're damn right," he exploded.

"And if you came close to a good girl, you might do something wrong?"

"I didn't say that. But . . . well, hell. Yes."

"Why would you do that, Will? Why?"

"Because I'm a man, that's why."

"No other reason?"

141

"Because . . . well, you're a hell of a gal."

"You think so, honest, Will?"

"I do."

"Then, you don't have to come over here."

Before he could answer she was alongside him on the blankets. She had removed the pretty dress and almost everything else. He could feel the softness and warmth of her and he could smell the clean, soapy odor of her. Around his neck the strong arms were firm and demanding, her face was rubbing against his. From her lips came a little humming sound that may have been a chuckle and may have been something else.

In his ear she finally whispered, "I love you, Will. Am I a bad girl for saying that I love you?"

Now he knew enough not to answer. It had never happened to him before, he knew he should not allow it to happen now. He was Carney, the gunslinger, and he was on the run, he was always on the run. But he folded her tight against him and babbled like a boy on his first picnic with his first girl.

Chapter Fourteen

LATE THE FOLLOWING afternoon the horses were saddled, the cabin was boarded up, and it was time to depart. They kissed, long and deep, in the doorway.

She said, "Oh, Will, I'm shameless, I'm a shameless woman."

He said, "When we get to the fort, you'll be my wife. And nobody, not anybody, calls my wife names!"

He kissed her again and slapped her on the firm behind, and they closed the door, leaving the latch string out for some other travelers who might need shelter.

Then they rode for Cibicu Creek, with Carney's rifle ready in the boot and his revolver on his hip lest the

Eggerlys come too quickly, at a time like this, the worst of all possible times.

As they rode he said, "You'll like Riley. He's old and tough and mean, but he's your friend for life."

"I've never been in Mexico," she said. There was an uncertain note in her voice. "I'm sure it will be fine if you say so."

"It'll be *hiyu* fine," he told her. "No Eggerlys."

"That's right. No Eggerlys, no more trouble."

The day darkened into dusk, and they finally saw the camp of the troops from the 6th Cavalry in the distance. Carney slowed down. Somehow he hated to go among people again right now. She smiled at him, a bit tremulous, and he felt a great surge of warmth toward her.

They rode together, and then he saw that something was wrong in the camp. There were too many Apaches in the vicinity. Men walked with their guns in their hands, patrolling. Three troopers stood guard over the seated, hunched form of Nok-e-da-klinne. The ugly Mosby was among the Indians from the reservation. Sergeant Smith was talking with Captain Hentig.

Dusk was coming softly to the Cibicu Creek area, and Carney drew rein, watching closely. Now he saw that the scouts had removed themselves from the troops and were in a camp of their own, and that reservation Apaches were moving in that direction, over a hundred of them, armed with guns and bows and arrows.

He said sharply to Betsy, "Turn around and get back to the cabin. There's going to be trouble here."

"But, Will," she protested. He swung Star around, reached out, and slapped the bay on the flank.

"Wait in the cabin for me!"

She was gone back up the trail. He sat one moment looking after her. Then the first shots rang out, and he was riding for the conflict.

The scouts had mutinied on an impulse because Nok-e-da-klinne was a medicine man and because they were, after all, Indians. The bunch from the reservation held the bulk of those who believed in their spiritual leader. The first barrage was terribly successful.

143

Carney, riding, saw Captain Hentig fall as Smith hit the dirt and began levering his carbine. The Apaches were advancing with wild yells. The troops, not entirely unprepared, scattered after the first volley. Six men were down with the Captain, but Lieutenant Carter, a young and dashing West Pointer, was cool, shouting orders as Sergeant Smith stood firm with blazing gun.

Carney went in on the flank. He was the only mounted man in the engagement. He rode hard, his rifle ready, got in close, and began firing from the saddle, one hand working the repeater, the butt cuddled beneath his arm. He saw Apache scouts he recognized—Deadshot, Dandy Jim, Skitashe. These three were sneaking through the heavy general firing with definite purpose, he thought. He rode straight through, bullets singing around him from the weapons of both parties.

It was a sharp fight, as bitter as he had ever seen. Star's nostrils were wide with fear as he danced while Carney reloaded the rifle and then drew his revolver for close work, preparing to make another run. Indians and troopers were still falling, the yells and noise of gunshots were wild on the soft evening air.

Now the troopers showed their mettle. Discipline prevailed, they made their stand around Lieutenant Carter. Carney came riding and then saw the three Apache mutineers. They were making a concerted dash to free Nok-e-da-klinne. There was space enough to ride, and Carney drove Star into it. He could see it all clearly despite the waning light.

Bugler Ahrens, a youth detailed to watch the Apache medicine man, saw at once what was up, thought that Deadshot and the others had a chance to make good their design. Carney came thundering, yipping to draw attention.

Skitashe was going in with a knife to cut Nok-e-da-klinne loose. Carney shot him in the back, but the others kept going, closing in. Bugler Ahrens lifted his heavy Army pistol. As Carney rode he saw Ahrens fire three times—into the head of the old medicine man.

Deadshot and Dandy Jim fell back, horrified. It would have been easy to cut them down, but Carney merely rode at them, forcing them to turn and run. There had been enough damage, he thought. He dismounted at the side of Sergeant Smith, rifle in one hand, revolver in the other. A bullet carried away his hat. He retrieved it, shrugged at the nick in its crown.

Smith said, "I told Cruse this'd happen."

"Too bad. Close work like this, you lose people."

"Should've left the old man alone."

"The old man's down," said Carney.

"Good thing. You can't just put 'em in jail. Not the medicine men. You got to scotch 'em like they're snakes," rejoined Smith, his face hard as flint. "Leave 'em alone or kill 'em."

They were firing at retreating Apaches now. The shooting of Nok-e-da-klinne took the fight from them, they had no reason to continue, Carney thought. They were far from stupid despite their superstitions. They would not fight without a reason.

Lieutenant Carter ordered a cease-fire. The troops stared around, a bit dazed. Nine of them were dead or nearly so, including their Captain. It had happened like a clap of thunder. Apaches lay in odd positions, a dozen left behind in the swift retreat, all dead.

The Lieutenant set a guard and ordered a burial detail to get to work, intent on preserving morale, keeping the men busy. Sergeant Smith looked to his weapons.

Carney said, "I'll have to go back and get the girl. See you on the road . . . where we met this morning."

"We won't be goin' that way now," said Smith. "Meet us at the old cutoff near the Cotton Rock."

"Okay," said Carney. He whistled, and Star came trotting to him. He started to mount, then said, "Good Lord, Smitty, look!"

Nok-e-da-klinne, his head bleeding, his eyes staring, death stalking him, was crawling on hands and knees. The Apache instinct was drawing him toward the reservation, toward his own people. Inch by inch he bled his way in the dirt.

"The poor bastard," growled Smith. "He didn't deserve this."

The Sergeant drew his pistol and aimed with great care. The single shot drew everyone's attention. The bullet struck into the brain of the old medicine man and finished him, this time forever. Smith strode to the body and stared at it. Then he reached down and took a chain from the neck of the Apache. He walked back to Carney extending a bronze medal.

"How about this?"

Carney turned the disc to the last of the failing light. It was a peace medal from a commission in Washington.

"Yeah," he said. "How about that?"

He handed it back, half saluted Smith, and mounted. He had one thought now, to get back with Betsy. The moon was rising, it would be full tonight. He wanted to cease thinking about anything but the girl he was going to marry. He had to get used to that idea, marriage.

He could not, however, refrain from thinking of Nok-e-da-klinne as he rode through the bright night. The medicine man had committed depredations, had misled his followers, had been wrong. But his one ambition had been to help his people. Right or wrong, he did not deserve the grisly fate that had been his finish.

It came down to murder. The Apache was unarmed, a prisoner when Ahrens shot him . . . and for this the bugler would probably get a medal. On the other hand, the death of the mystic leader had certainly ended the hostilities at Cibicu Creek and saved other lives. There were many matters in the world, Carney decided, for which he had no easy solution.

Such as taking Betsy into Mexico, a new and strange land to her, as the wife of a working man. Riley was his friend, but it would be a start at the bottom of the ladder. Was it right to take the girl to that sort of life, all hard work and no frills? He had asked her right out, and she had replied that nothing mattered so long as they were married.

But it would matter sooner or later, he reasoned. It had to if she was human. She was a ranch girl, true, but her folks had owned their spread. It made a big difference if a man had land of his own.

Resentment against being driven from Arizona rose within him. The Eggerlys . . . if it were not for them, he could make a new start in his own part of the country,

146

live down his reputation with his marriage. Others had done it.

He rode through moonlight smooth as silk, pondering. The night was balmy, it was no time for regrets, he told himself, no time for looking backward. A future with this woman of his choice lay ahead, and whatever the obstacles, they would face them with courage as long as they were together. It was a brilliant new thing with Carney, something in which to luxuriate, putting aside all doubt.

A home, he thought, wherever they went, whatever they did, they would have a home. She had shown him with a few gestures in the cabin on the hilltop what it meant to have a place with a woman in it. He had wondered to see how her every move made such a difference, marveled at the easy grace of her and her strength past his understanding.

The riding and the gambling and the whoring up and down the land were a closed chapter. Here was new life indeed, a way of living on which he had never dreamed. It was Betsy who had opened the door, shown him the way and lain in his arms, murmuring to him so that he shivered to remember the tenderness and wonder of it all.

Star sucked wind, no more than a small intake, but Carney knew instantly that he had pushed the willing horse too far and too fast. He reined in, dismounted. The cabin lay just over the next hill, not more than half a mile. It might be wise to rest a moment, prepare himself, and let the big black take a blow.

He was at Star's head beside the road, his mind going ahead, looking ahead and upward as though he might get a glimpse of the cabin wherein Betsy would be waiting, futile from this place. In that instant moonlight glinted on a rifle barrel.

Instantly he was into the deep shadows of heavy brush. He had been night-dreaming, he had momentarily lost that sixth sense of the hunted man that had always served him well. He trailed the bridle rein, unshipped his rifle, and whispered to Star. Then he was making his way up the hill by small, inching moves. Apache teaching had lingered in him, he had never lost the skills they had given him.

The man with the gun was a lookout, all right. He was nestled down beside a boulder, heading toward the road that Carney had just deserted. Another moment or two and it would have been too late.

The situation was clear as the light of the moon. If a man was lying in wait to sound an alarm or to ambush him, then Betsy was a captive. The Eggerlys had finally caught up with him.

Blood ran cold, then hot in Carney's veins. He foggily fought for control as he wormed his way, snakelike, into position, making a circle to come up behind the rock where the sentry slouched, leaning hard against the rock, perhaps not fully awake, certainly not expecting attack. All the mountainside was quiet, not a breeze stirred.

Carney came around with the rifle barrel, using it whiplike against the man's head, then nailing him to earth. He stared down into the face of a stranger, a bearded countenance now bloody and frightened. The man was in middle years, there was a scar above his left eye.

Carney growled, "Where's Simon Eggerly?"

The man's voice was hoarse, deep in his beard, "At . . . at the cabin."

"He's got the girl?"

"Yeah, he's got the girl."

"How many men?"

"Eighteen, countin' me."

"Seventeen now."

"If you'd gimme a start," the man begged.

The safe thing to do was to knife him and leave him here, out of it, Carney knew. If they had hurt Betsy . . . But he could not do it now, somehow or other.

"You got a horse?"

"In the brush, there."

"All right. Let's see you ride."

The man stood up, wiped blood from his scarred brow. "I tell you, Carney, I don't like it about the girl."

"They hurt her?" His hands were shaking despite himself.

148

"She fought. They roughed her some. I can't side you, Carney. As it is, if Simon ever gets me, you know what'll happen. But I don't like it about the girl. He'll hang you and her, too."

"He won't hang me."

"There's seventeen of 'em. I'd go in the back way, over the hill, I was you. High-gun 'em. At that, they got her, and what can you do?"

"I can take a lot of 'em along with me," said Carney. "Simon Eggerly, I'll take him along."

"I wish you luck, at that. You're goin' to plumb need it."

"Ride," Carney told him. "Ride fast and don't come back."

The man went down the hill and in a moment he was riding toward Cibicu Creek. He would not turn back, Carney thought, you could always tell when they had enough and would keep running. That left seventeen. And they had Betsy.

He began to go over the hilltop and along the side of the mountain, knowing his way, having that small advantage, familiar with this part of the range. He would be going past the digging that had not panned out and then straight ahead until the cabin was below him. If the moonlight held, it would be bad for him.

Simon Eggerly would kill the girl, there was no question about that. The old man was full of hate, and murder was nothing in his lexicon, especially when it related to the death of his son Bud. In Simon's mind the girl would be partially responsible, she would be the harpy who teased the boy into passion, then rejected him. Carney had to think hard on that point: Simon would kill Betsy Gaye.

In the past week life had moved very swiftly, he went on in his mind, snaking past an organ pipe cactus growing incongruously on the hill. He had left Tombstone with casual plans for the immediate future in Sautelle, there had been nothing important in prospect, it had been a case of merely keeping out of the way of the Eggerlys. He had run into trouble . . . and Betsy. And now that life was worth the cost of the effort, now

149

that the future was made of great and wonderful plans, it suddenly came to an ending.

Nok-e-da-klinne, he thought, had won their duel. The fact of the medicine man's death had put Betsy in Simon Eggerly's hands and brought Carney to this forlorn last stand. It was a tricky world, first, last, and all the time.

He went a devious way, walking a narrow ledge for a quarter mile between the old diggings and the cabin. He was caught in the light of the moon against the rock, hung there for a minute as he inched along, being monstrously careful of his rifle and his gunbelt and sheathed knife lest they make a sound to attract the attention of those below. He kept his mind occupied with the minutiae of his progress and refused to think about Betsy and what they might be doing to her.

A rock was dislodged above him, and he froze in the rays of the moon, waiting for it to come down and strike him and knock him off the ledge. It skipped past him and went into the gorge, and then he thought there would be rifle fire and he dropped to a knee, ready for it.

Then a mountain lion sent its weird cry echoing, and down by the cabin there was unrest but no sound of rifles. Carney moved again, his hands cramped and damp. He wiped his fingers on his rebosa and began the descent. This was the most difficult of all, each step bringing him nearer to his goal, each step risking more than the previous one.

When he came to the stream, he was south of the clearing. He made his way, crawling, then running in a stooped posture, then crawling again, to the rock where he had sunned himself with Betsy. He remembered her shapely brown hands, so useful, now so dear to him, and he shuddered, gathering himself, sliding onto the rock where he could see them and not be seen.

Seventeen of them, he thought, and impossible even in the bright moonlight to keep them all in his line of vision. He knew what he must do, it was all plain to him, but he wished he could see them all. He stood upon the rock for a moment unobserved, seeking his target.

150

Then he levered his rifle, and at that unmistakable clicking sound they all stayed where they were, unstirring, gaping up at him. He trained the muzzle of the gun upon Simon Eggerly and said as quietly as possible. "This thing goes off no matter what happens. You know who'll get killed."

There were plenty of them sprawled around, waiting for him, he could not count how many. He saw Paul Eggerly over at the door of the cabin. Simon was standing near his son but apart from them all, as was his prideful custom. It made him an excellent target.

"You shoot, and the girl dies," Simon roared. "Bring her out, you in there, bring her out!"

They forced her ahead of them, Sim Martin and Sanchez, the pair from Tucson. Her clothing was torn, and Carney thought he could see bruises upon her. Her head was high, and they had been forced to tie her hands to keep her from fighting them.

She called at once, "Never mind me, Will. Do what you have to do."

Carney said, "Cut her loose. Give her the bay horse."

"You think I'm crazy?" howled Simon Eggerly. "You throw down your guns, or Sanchez'll put his knife into her."

Carney could see the knife then, aimed at Betsy's back. He began to feel the gorge rising. He had told himself a hundred times on his journey to this place that he must not let the blood get hot, he must fight that familiar feeling that embraced him in a tight, he must make them see that his way was the only way, that they had to do as he demanded.

He said, "The second bullet will be for Sanchez."

"You got no chance," Simon Eggerly said. "There's guns on you right now."

"Before they down me, you'll be dead, and Sanchez will be dead," Carney told him, managing very well with his voice. "You know that. You know it damn good."

Eggerly said, "So I'll die. You'll follow me to hell in the next breath, Carney."

151

"It's your choice," Carney told him. "You better listen to me."

"I'm going to hang you, Carney. Dead or alive, I'm going to have you strung up."

"That's of no matter to me," Carney said. "I'm telling you to turn the girl loose or I'll finish you. And if you do, I'll throw down my rifle and take my chances."

"You think I believe that?" demanded Simon Eggerly.

"I keep sayin' it's your choice." Carney's rifle never wavered, they knew his skill, his quickness. He held down on them from above and waited.

Sanchez whispered, "Don't do it, señor. Allow me to kill this woman."

Paul Eggerly moved. His voice was stolidly clear. "You better do like he says. I believe him."

"Shut up, you bullhead," Simon Eggerly raved. "You damn fool, you'd have let the girl go before now. You're part woman yourself, you booby."

Paul said, "Maybe, but I don't favor hurtin' girls."

"Nobody gives a hoot in hell what you favor," thundered his father. "Carney!"

"I'm waitin'."

"You throw down your rifle and your pistol, and I'll think about lettin' the gal loose."

"You're pretty funny sometimes, you know that?" Carney made himself laugh lightly. "I'm not givin' you much more time, Eggerly. You heard Betsy. If we got to go, we're takin' you along."

"I won't do it!"

Eggerly looked right, then left, his lips moving, cursing his son Paul, cursing Betsy and Carney, cursing the guard who had let Carney by, cursing the world.

Sim Martin said timidly, "Cousin, we can get the gal later, whenever we want to."

"Yeah," said someone in the shadows near the cabin. "We'll find her, wherever she goes to."

Eggerly stared around, inhaled, waving his arms. "You all want to let her go, is that it?"

"Not I, señor," Sanchez answered.

152

"You're a good man, but what's the use? Chicken livers, we got. Yella chicken livers. Carney!"

"You've got about three seconds," Carney said. "I'm gettin' real itchy-fingered up here when I look at that Sanchez."

Eggerly said, "You'll throw down your guns when I let her go?"

"I'll throw down the rifle and take my chances. That lets you off the hook. There's seventeen of you and one of me. Figure it out, Eggerly. Is it worth it?"

"If I had a man with the guts to shoot you down offen that rock . . ." Simon Eggerly broke off. He looked at Sanchez and said, "Cut her loose."

"But, señor . . ."

"Cut her loose, I said."

Sanchez hesitated. Carney flicked the muzzle of the gun, fired, immediately retrained it upon Simon Eggerly. The bullet spun Sanchez in a circle and slammed him against the cabin, where he screamed in agony from the pain of the shattered arm.

Carney said, "He's too free with that knife. Maybe you better try it, Martin."

The Tucson marshal gingerly severed the bonds holding Betsy's wrists together. She began chafing her hands, restoring circulation, looking up at Carney, trying to figure the next move, not speaking, not objecting or rejoicing, thinking it through as she always did.

"The bay horse," Carney said.

Someone brought it, another man saddled it. From the cabin they produced her belongings, securing them to the saddle. Eggerly stood, a gross figure, glowering, lusting for the bloodbath to follow.

Carney called, "Good-bye, Betsy."

She climbed aboard, disdaining to cover her long, lovely legs, sitting astride. She looked up at him and lifted her right hand and said, "Good-bye, darling . . . and thanks."

"Ride to Fort Apache," he said. "Sergeant Smith is your man. He'll take care of Eggerlys or anyone who tries to bother you."

153

"Good-bye, good-bye," she wept, and rode toward the trail leading down from the hill.

Eggerly was already crying, "Throw it down, Carney, drop them guns."

"I promised the rifle," Carney said. "And only after she gets a start. Follow her to the fort and see what happens to you, you bigmouthed bastard."

"Throw it down, Carney. You said you'd throw it down."

Carney waited until he could not hear the sound of the bay horse any longer. The good little mount would take her to Sergeant Smith, they could not catch her now. Then he stood very straight in the moonlight. It was almost as bright as day.

He yelled, "Here you are, Eggerly," and threw the gun hard toward the big man. At the same instant he drew his revolver and slid down from the rock on the far side, and the bullets began to rain like hailstones around him.

He remained very still as they continued shooting. If he exposed a hand, it would be shot off. He let them fire round after round before he took the chance he had been planning.

He came around the rock crouched, with his pistol in his hand. He fired once, twice, then ran for the protection of the cabin. He saw Sim Martin go down and another, shadowy, unknown, howled and died. Eggerly was somewhere out of view. Paul stood beside the cabin, as though bemused.

Carney shoved fresh shells into his revolver and moved again. Three down, fourteen to go, and how many could he hope to take before they got him and put a rope around his neck?

Someone spotted him in the shadows and yelled and fired, and Eggerly bellowed for a charge. There was really no place to run to.

Carney did not want to die, not yet. He ran around the house. Two men tried to intercept him, and he picked them off, dodging, unhurt for that time.

He came around close to Paul Eggerly. He saw Simon now in the shelter of the trees. He ran behind

Paul and then past him to the door of the cabin. He spun and fired at Eggerly. Simon snapped his pistol.

Paul fell back, saying calmly, without surprise, "You've shot me, Pa."

"Get the hell outa the way," his father roared.

"But you shot me. You didn't care. You just shot me." It was a statement, as though Paul knew it would come to this and only had been awaiting the time.

Carney was halfway inside the cabin, firing at two men who were at its windows with rifles. They fell, and Carney turned again, catching up one of the Remingtons, looking for Simon.

It was then that Betsy Gaye appeared. She was on the periphery of the action and she had the ridiculous little two-shot derringer in her hand. She was also searching out Simon, moving with caution, her skirt caught up between her thighs, her face luminous in the moonlight.

Carney groaned. It was all lost now. She had refused to leave him, doubled back under cover of the firing, and now they would get her.

He banged off several rounds toward Simon's position and then broke for the place where he could see Betsy among the stunted fir trees. At least they could die side by side, he thought. He ran past Paul Eggerly without thought. Simon was firing at him, the combined guns were all thundering, and the lead pelted past his ears, his legs.

Then he caught a glimpse of Paul Eggerly with a shotgun in his hands. He heard Paul yell. He dove into the scant cover, calling to Betsy to stay put and wait for him.

Behind him Paul Eggerly said again, "Stop! Stop this, all of you."

His father shouted, "Shut up, you fool!"

Paul called, "I'll shoot the next man that fires a gun. This is murder. I'm sick of this."

Simon Eggerly came into view now. He had a rifle in one hand and a long-barreled Colt in the other. He yelled, "You're not fit to carry my name!"

Paul faced him. Carney lifted his revolver, but

155

Betsy was at his side, clinging to him, whispering, "Wait, they've forgotten us."

Simon fired the first shot. Then Paul pulled the trigger of the shotgun.

Paul went down. Simon staggered back three steps, then doubled over. He was dead on the instant.

Carney's voice pealed above the echoes, "That'll do it. The rest of you come out and shower down."

They came, hesitating, their eyes not upon Carney but upon father and son lying in their blood. There were cousins and in-laws among them but no one from Sautelle, these were the remnants of the bunch Simon had driven up and down the Territory seeking Carney. They gathered in a knot, and he counted them to make sure, even then knowing the war was over, that the impetus behind it all was gone, that this was the final curtain for the Eggerly clan and its domination over Arizona.

And as they watched, Paul raised himself on one elbow. There was blood on him, but his voice was amazingly clear and strong.

"You all saw it. He tried to kill me."

"He did, Paul, he did," a man muttered.

"I'd never of believed it," said another.

"His own son. He made Paul shoot him."

Paul continued, "There's buryin' to do. And then we ride."

Carney came in then, alert, ready for anything. Betsy ran to kneel beside the wounded young man, and they all murmured again, as though dazed, not understanding that she had come back or why, bemused.

Carney said, "Easy does it."

"It's all right," Paul told him as Betsy tore at her petticoat to make a bandage to staunch the blood that ran from his chest. "I mean you, Carney, it's all right about you. Bud had it comin' for years. Pa had no right. None of us had right."

The others shuffled their feet, silent under the quiet and calm voice. Carney holstered his gun, and the slick sound was plain to be heard in the mountain stillness.

Betsy said, "Get him in the cabin. He can live if we attend to him."

156

Paul was a heavy man, it was with difficulty that they picked him up. Betsy ran to them, cautioning them, directing them, and they listened to her gravely, obeying.

From the shadows Sanchez screamed once more. "Traitors! This shall not be!"

Carney turned and drew. He saw Sanchez lift a rifle and made the first shot quick, at the body, then sent the second on its course as Sanchez whirled, the flash of his rifle like a small celebration, a Fourth of July rocket toward the sky, a period, a complete ending to it all.

Moonlight flooded the clearing, and each man looked at the others and was startled to see how different everything had become at the ending.

Paul Eggerly called weakly, "Carney . . . Carney . . . It's going to be different now . . ."

A man said, "Paul's right. Simon was wrong. That Bud never was no good. I dunno why I folloyed Simon like I did."

And Carney saw them with new eyes, plain men who belonged back at their ranches, their farms, wherever their families waited and worried. He said, "Simon was that kind of man. He was a leader. There can be good men who are leaders. I'd pin my faith in Paul."

Then he went into the cabin, and Betsy was bending over the burly Eggerly scion. Carney went for a basin, paused, kissed the nape of her neck, not caring who saw him. There had been no possible escape, yet they had survived, and he well knew that a small miracle had taken place in this spot where he had found the meaning of life and love and new hope.

Chapter Fifteen

CHARLES MARGATE SAID, "Madge, you shouldn't attempt it. You can look out the window."

"You're helping me," she told him. "We're going fine. Stop worrying."

They came slowly onto the verandah of the hotel, and Milton was hopping around with pillows under his arms. The newly arrived doctor, a very young man named Samuelson, from Denver, was standing by, not approving but unwilling to force the lady to remain in bed when she was so determined.

Mr. Brand was waiting, nodding, already in position beside another chair. Ed Leeds waved from the general store. Chico, the bartender of the Cowboy Saloon, had slicked his hair down and donned a shirt of loud stripes. Marshal Dan Shriver came bustling up and said, "Y'all are just in time. They're comin' down the road now."

The walks were lined with curious people, miners, ranchers, cowboys, and a few blanket Indians. Dogs scampered and barked, and children clamored. It was holiday time in Sautelle.

An Army ambulance hove into view, pulled by four mules. A trooper drove, and there was a white-jacketed attendant beside him. Charles Margate went down the steps, using one cane but walking straight and strong. Then someone yelled, "There they are! Look at 'em!"

Betsy Gaye wore her favorite gray and rode side-saddle. Alongside her was Carney, in his new clothing, a dark suit purchased at Fort Apache, pants rounded like a stovepipe, his boots shined to mirror gloss, his hat cocked to one side.

Behind them rode the Eggerly clan, those from the Sautelle area and those who had not gone home from the cabin in the mountains where they had buried Simon and his followers who had died of bullet wounds. They, too, were attired in their Sunday-go-to-meeting clothing and their families followed in carriages and wagons.

Madge wept a little and said, "Betsy looks so sweet and lovely."

Milton crowed, "Look at Carney, how he rides, so tall in the saddle."

The ambulance pulled up, and Dr. Samuelson went down to the rear. The Eggerlys, however, dismounted and marched forward, gently shoving everyone else aside.

158

They reached into the ambulance, and Bo tugged at a stretcher, and then Peter and Jack and the attendant managed to haul out the bulk of Paul and gingerly angle him up the steps and onto the verandah, where they deposited him while they got a new grip on him to carry him to the room the Margates had prepared.

"Eve'thing ready?" demanded Bo.

"The telegram was very explicit," said Madge. "He'll be comfortable."

Paul needed a shave, but his eyes were clear. "Want to thank you, Mrs. Margate, ma'am, seein' as you yourself ain't feelin' so good."

"Don't thank me, we are running a hotel."

"But you offered," he said earnestly. "I 'preciate that, offerin' to take in an Eggerly."

"You stood up to your father," she reminded him, speaking softly for his ears alone. "That's the point. Not what happened. That you stood up to him."

"Thank you again, ma'am," Paul said, and then they got their holds on the stretcher and took him inside, Dr. Samuelson following, looking worried.

Madge Margate looked up to see Betsy and Carney coming toward her. She coughed once, then recovered. She said, "Well . . . you two. Reverend will be here any minute. You're sure you want to be married here?"

The townspeople were gathering. Reverend Peterson could be seen coming from the church, stately, tin-lipped, disapproving mildly of this unconventional idea.

Betsy said, "It's better than moving you all the way down the street to those uncomfortable pews. And who else would stand up with me?"

"Anyone in town. Especially the Eggerly women," Madge told her. "They're a strange clan. They are very glad to be rid of Simon. But look how they flock to Paul, the new leader."

Dan Shriver, hat in hand, nodded agreement. "Seein' I was married to one, I got to say that's the way they are. Like they need somebody at the top to holler on."

"Paul's a good man," said Carney. He looked at Betsy, then addressed Madge. "We were headin' for Mexico. Paul called us to the hospital at the fort. Said there's a spread near Sautelle here that could be improved. Said he always wanted to stock it with some Herefords and see what happened. Said a man could own it after a while."

"He felt the Eggerlys owed us a start," Betsy explained. "Will didn't want to take it. But he decided."

"We decided," said Carney. "There's two of us now."

Dan Shriver fidgeted, then blurted, "We got plans, too. We just formed a county seat. When the legislature meets, we'll be needin' a sheriff. Me, I aim to stick to farmin' from now on, maybe bein' the marshal won't take all the time it did." He grinned. "It didn't take that much time if Farber didn't want all that attention. We figured you'd be a fine sheriff, Carney."

Reverend Peterson was ascending the steps, his Bible under his arm. Carney looked around him at the people of Sautelle, all solemn for the occasion, all their faces turned to Betsy and to him, friendly, open, already accepting him.

"Whatever," said Carney. "Whatever my neighbors want. A man's been runnin' so long, he's grateful to have neighbors."

He took his place beside Betsy to be married on the verandah of the hotel, with the whole town a part of it. Milton stumbled in with an armful of wild flowers and put them where the Reverend waited. Charles Margate fumbled for the plain gold ring, and all the men removed their hats. Betsy took his arm, and Carney blinked his eyes to clear away the mist and listened to the words of the simple service. He would run no more, he knew.

70-4-2

William R. Cox was born in Peapack, New Jersey. His early career was in newspaper journalism. In the late 1930s he began writing sports, crime and adventure stories for the magazine market, and he made his debut as a Western writer with 'Night of the Blood Bucket Raid' in *Dime Western* in the January, 1941 issue. It is worth noting that his Western story debut was with the first of several stories to feature a series character, Terry Glenn. During the 1940s Cox created a number of other series characters for the magazine market, most notably the Whistler Kid who appeared regularly in *10 Story Western* and Duke Bagley whose adventures usually were featured in *Star Western*. 'The short story form was blissful until there were no markets,' he once recalled. In the 1950s and 1960s Cox turned to television and wrote at least a hundred teleplays for such series as 'Broken Arrow,' 'Dick Powell's Zane Grey Theatre,' 'The Virginian,' and 'Bonanza.' He also won a host of readers writing original paperback Western novels, the best known of which are novels about the adventures of two series characters originally published by Fawcett Gold Medal: Cemetery Jones in a series published under his own byline and the Tom Buchanan series which appeared under the house name, Jonas Ward. Dale L. Walker in the second edition of *Twentieth Century Western Writers* (1991) commented that William R. Cox's Western 'novels are noted for their "page-turner" pace, realistic dialogue, and frequent Colt-and-Winchester gun play. The series of novels built around the strong West Texas character, Tom Buchanan, are very typical Cox Westerns.' Among his non-series Western novels, his most notable titles are *Comanche Moon* (1959), *The Gunsharp* (1965), and *Moon at Cobre* (1969).